A Soldier's Vow
Angelica Kate

Cover by: Liz Seils
Editing: Jill Uppendahl

Angelica Kate
© 2015 Angela K. Naff

PROLOGUE

May 10, 2013

Lane was trying to focus on finishing the report in front of him. He had promised the client to have it completed and emailed over before close of business. Glancing at the clock for the fifteenth time in less than five minutes, he gave up forcing himself to concentrate and picking up the cell phone lying on his desk, tried again to reach Sarah.

Three rings and then the message he knew by heart, *"You've reached Sarah Gettner, please leave a message and I'll get back to you in a jiffy!"* BEEP!

"Sarah, please call me back as soon as you get this. I'm worried sick, and the news isn't helping," he stated brusquely.

He sighed knowing the panic was evident in his voice. He slid his finger over the face of the phone disconnecting the call. Verifying on his watch that it was nearly time to go pick up Sophie, he tried again to concentrate on the report displayed on his computer. His mind wandered again. He knew the schools went into lockdown when the threat of tornados or other bad weather was broadcasted, but Sarah always called as soon as the kids were taken care of after such a threat, to let him know things were back to normal. Today though his stomach was churning violently telling him something was wrong.

A knock interrupted his train of thought. Looking up, he smiled when he saw Sydney standing in the door.

"Did you take a look at the space?" he asked genuinely interested in something other than his growing dread.

"Yeah, I think it will work great, and it would be wonderful for Clementine to be so close to Jett, especially once they are married. Although, I'm a bit worried they won't get any work done," she said, with a telling stain creeping up her cheeks.

Clementine and Sydney still had several months left of interning with Dr. Bershaw, but they were already starting to set the wheels in motion for their own practice. He and Jett had finally pooled their resources in the last three months and purchased a building to house their security firm. The bonus to the structure was it featured another roomy office space that would be perfect for the counseling center Clementine and Sydney would be operating. They had agreed that sharing the expenses would allow both new businesses to breathe a bit easier as they got established.

He couldn't help but observe how far Sydney had come from the frightened young woman he had plucked out of that shack in an old mining camp in Peru. She and Clementine had been taken hostage by a local military group and held with a group of others in the hot, rundown cabin while volunteering with an orphanage during their summer break from college. He and Jett had volunteered to be part of the extraction teams sent in to get them. He remembered his first triage assessment of Sydney when they managed to subdue the militants and rescue the hostages. She had a terrible gash that ran down her leg that without treatment had become septic, and she had been nearly delirious from the infection. She was half starved yet her first concern had been for her friend, and it wasn't until she heard that Jett had Clementine that she had succumbed to unconsciousness. That scary episode had not only proven their women's mettle but also forced

Jett and Clementine to acknowledge their feelings for each other.

Lane chuckled, thinking about Clementine and Jett's very public displays of affection in recent months. They had a way of looking at each other that reminded him of similar moments all the way back in high school between Sarah and him. It seemed like just yesterday and yet they had been together for close to fifteen years.

"You might be right about Clementine and Jett," he replied, not able to stop his eyes from wandering to the phone.

"Haven't you heard from any of them? I know Sarah normally calls when they get the all clear, but I didn't check the weather to see how bad things were out that way," she said, biting her lip worriedly.

"I heard from Jett and Clementine. They finished their inspection but took an alternate route to avoid the worst of the weather. You know Jett's opinion of the crazy driver's when the roads get slick. I haven't been able to reach Sarah though. The school must be on lockdown," he said, attempting to keep his voice even and to not concern Sydney.

Unfortunately, looking at the weather, it appeared to be on a collision course with the small town in which his wife taught. Logically, he knew the weather personnel often overstated the danger to ensure people took precautions, and often it didn't turn out nearly as bad as they predicted.

"How many times have you tried calling her?"

"Six," he said, giving her a sheepish look. "Overkill you think?"

"No, I'd feel lucky if someone cared that much about me," she said wistfully.

"Sydney, one of these days, you are going to find someone great." He meant every word of the compliment. She was intelligent and hard-working, but more than that, she had heart. Someone like that wouldn't be single for long.

She inhaled deeply and averted her eyes. He knew it was a touchy subject. In the year plus that he had known Clementine, and Sydney by extension as her best friend, he had never seen the woman show any interest in a guy. She was pretty with her gentle brown eyes, light brown hair and slim figure. On the other hand, she did nothing to enhance herself and preferred a simple minimalist approach to dress and make-up that didn't initially draw a man. However, if someone took the time to draw her out, she was a good conversationalist and as kindhearted as his own wife.

Thinking of Sarah caused him to check the phone one more time. Nothing!

"Lane, it's only been…"

The door flew open. Clementine followed by an out of breath Jett stumbled in to the room. The look on both of their faces elevated his concern past the panic level.

"Did you see the news?" Clementine panted, bending over at the knees trying to catch her breath.

"No. Why?" He felt the spike in adrenaline hit him like a hard punch to the gut.

"Lane, we need to go...now!" Jett said simply.

Looking at his best friend's face he knew something was horribly wrong. Jett had worked in combat zones so he wasn't prone to hysterics, but after surviving the worst of situations together, he could read the man like an open book.

"Sophie?" he looked at Sydney.

"I have her, go!" She often picked the baby up from daycare if he was busy and kept her until either he or Sarah could pick her up.

He hustled after Jett who wasn't speaking. The tense focused look on his face reminded Lane of the expression he got just before they moved into enemy territory on a dangerous mission. Lane couldn't help spinning tales in his head of worst case scenarios. Picking up his phone, he set to try Sarah's number again.

"Lane," Jett shook his head and stopped him with an outstretched hand.

A SOLDIER'S VOW -- 8

Putting the truck in gear, Jett spun out onto the road at a rate of speed that would cover the short thirty-mile distance in minutes. His sweet Sarah had to be okay, no matter what had spooked Jett and Clementine. Their nine-month-old daughter needed her mother. They had plans for the future that were just now gaining momentum. After a decade in the military, he had finally retired to start the security firm with Jett that allowed him to be home full-time. Sarah and he were going to plant their garden this weekend, take Sophie to the zoo and spend time as a family. He shook his head. He was the level-headed one, the voice of reason. There was no need to panic. She had to be alright.

He heard the sirens in the distance and saw the lights breaking up the dark horizon. Looking out the side window he saw the stream of cars all on the other side of the road from the one they now traveled. It was as if everything slowed as Jett spanned the distance to the first barrier at a break neck speed. Pulling abreast of the police officer, he heard Jett tell them Lane's wife was a kindergarten teacher at the local elementary school. Lane saw the concern on the officer's face as he directed Jett to where he should proceed for additional information.

Lane was the soldier. *He* was the one that had made a career out of dangerous missions. As they drove forward, he saw the first obliterated houses and debris lying about as if carelessly tossed by a giant. In an instant, he was transported to places he should never have been that had looked like that. Locations his gentle, easy going wife had never even been told about. Places torn asunder by bombs, war and civil discord. But Sarah was teaching kindergarten, educating the tiny minds of tomorrow, and as he looked around a weight settled over him like lead. Tornados like combatants didn't care who you were or why you were there, they strike at will without concern for the physical and emotional destruction that they leave in their wake.

As they arrived at the make-shift command center, Lane exited the truck and felt his head hit his chest. There in front of them was a somber row of ambulances with their back doors open toward the rubble that had once been a school. He heard the screams of children being comforted all around him and wails of parents still not able to wrap their arms around a missing child. In that instant, as he looked around and listened to the sounds of fear and grief, he thought back to that morning and gratefully recalled kissing Sarah on her head and telling her he loved her before they had both gone about their daily routine. That at least was a small comfort amidst the numbness seeping into his heart.

CHAPTER 1

Nearly a year later

Sydney was transcribing notes as quickly as she could decipher her own handwriting on the notebook lying open next to her laptop. So deeply engrossed in the process, she never heard movement until Clementine plopped unceremoniously into the chair opposite her desk.

"Geez, you scared me!" She jumped in response to the sudden noise. She looked up at her best friend and business partner with half chastising, half inquisitive eyes.

"That was the intention. You seemed a bit too engrossed in that report you are writing," Clementine quirked a brow at her.

"Don't judge. I like to be thorough."

"Yes, I know, but I have so much on my mind that I can't focus on reports right now. Maybe I need to pay to sit on your couch for an hour," Clementine said with an exaggerated sigh.

"First off, you are a therapist just as I am. Maybe you should talk to yourself." She stopped, realizing how funny that sounded as it left her mouth.

"Aren't we supposed to heal those that hear and talk to…?"

"Voices," Sydney finished for her. "Yes, yes we are," she grimaced, closed her laptop and gave Clementine her undivided attention. "What's up?"

"Do you realize it is just over ten weeks until my wedding? We started our business in earnest only four months ago, and I expected it to be a bit slow at first, giving me time to get everything done. Today, I had calls taking our last new patient spots and putting clients on a wait list. That is not a gradual increase in my opinion," she finished the high pitched babbling with a shake of her head.

Sydney held up her hands, "Whoa, I think that was a couple concerns all rolled into one run on statement. First, I agree that we are doing much better than we anticipated when we were putting together first year projections for our business plan. Getting in with the Department of Health Services and certified to work with the children in their care was a good idea. I just didn't realize the volume it would bring in."

"Jett and Lane are just as busy. So between our two schedules I'm getting to see my fiancé for only small snippets of time at crazy strange hours," Clementine said, her bottom lip protruding like a petulant two-year old instead of a full-grown woman.

"Ah, that is how you smashed those two subjects together. So both of the businesses being so successful is making wedding planning hard?" She sometimes had to slowly process, pick apart conjoined thoughts, and regurgitate sentiments to Clementine who handled things at a much different rate. It was a trick that worked well on her clients and ensured Clementine and she remained on the same page.

"Yes!"

"What else is there to decide? You have everyone lined out in the wedding party, the location, date and the groom... I think you are set," she said supportively.

Clementine thought about that for a minute, "He is dreamy, isn't he?"

Another bad habit of Clementine's was to lose all focus on normal daily tasks whenever Jett came up in conversation. They had been friends long enough that

Sydney didn't begrudge her the happiness and for the most part had learned to play along.

"As I have told you every time that you have asked me that question, you seem like the ideal pair. I can't imagine anyone better for you, I am grateful he makes you so blissfully happy and you help smooth all his rough edges out," she said just a teensy bit enviously.

"But he's not Fletcher?" Clementine teased, again changing the subject so fast that Sydney had to take a minute in order to detour her brain onto the next topic.

Fletcher Miles was a pharmaceutical representative Sydney had met while working for Dr. Bershaw. For the first time in her life, she had immediately clicked with someone, and they had a wonderful time together. He was friendly, outgoing and able to overcome her more bashful personality with ease. They enjoyed similar passions, were both dedicated to their careers and agreed on a slow and steady courtship, just as she had always thought it should be, friendship first and then romantic intentions.

Fletcher was easy on the eyes in a suit and tie in a way that Jett would never have been able to pull off. He had sandy hair, the color of a warm beach, nice chocolate brown eyes and was perfectly tailored, whether dressing for the office, a night out or a casual get-together with friends.

Her only issue with the relationship was that he didn't have anything in common with Jett, Lane or Ryker, and she spent a lot of time with them and their wives and girlfriends. Those three were all ex-military, preferred jeans and t-shirts, contact sports and rowdy, boisterous cookouts in the backyard. Fletcher enjoyed nice restaurants, theater and organized social events where he could network. Sydney loved her expanded family by friendship and was hopeful that over time Fletcher would find more common ground with the guys, which would allow them to mesh social engagements better and not force her to continue to choose. She couldn't imagine always feeling torn between her friends and him when trying to plan her free time. Other than that, she couldn't imagine a better match for her personally.

"No, he is definitely not Fletcher," she said with a sigh.

"Everything good there?" Clementine asked sitting forward in the chair.

"Absolutely. I just wish that the guys had more in common with him because I love spending time with you all but sometimes it's just not his thing," she said with a small shrug.

"Sydney, all of us want you to be happy. If Fletcher is the man of your dreams and you love him, I promise we will too," Clementine said with a genuine smile.

"Thanks! Now back to this wedding issue. Is there anything I can help you with?"

"Be careful what you ask for," Clementine said with a twinkle in her eye.

Sydney knew she wasn't going to like what came next, but what were best friends for if not to help carry the load for each other?

*****

Lane hit the conference phone button to disconnect the call, and rotating his shoulders, sat back in his chair covering his eyes with his hands. He inhaled and exhaled in slow steady breaths, allowing just a single quiet moment to gather his nerves. The call was exactly the announcement he had been hoping for and dreading in turn.

"That is good and bad news, I guess," Jett said intruding on his mini-break.

"Yeah, it's a huge contract for us and could be a huge boon for our business. Problem is I have no one to leave Sophie with for a week."

"I know for a fact that Clementine would help," Jett said tentatively.

Lane worried that Clementine had enough on her plate. She and Jett were busy planning their impending nuptials, to say nothing of the fact that she and Sydney were working overtime to get their own small business up and running. On the other hand, Sydney was always willing to pick up and watch Sophie when he asked, so maybe between the two of them it would be manageable? He would need to think of a big thank you gift for that level of help, as he knew the two would never accept payment. The thought definitely had merit and would cross his biggest concern regarding the new contract off his list.

"Also, we would need Ryker to agree. And we would have to have at least two sub-contractors to pull it off."

"Yeah, I was going to run down my usual list of suspects and see what I can come up with. You will need to try and pry Ryker from his adoring bride, but I think you might be able to talk him into giving us six days," Jett said with a cheeky grin.

"Since I have to knock on the office door before entering because of you and your chosen, I don't think you should be the one casting stones," Lane tried to maintain a stern look his buddy's direction.

"One time! It was only once you caught us…"

"Aghhh!" Lane held up his hands to stop him. "I know what I saw, no need to re-live it."

Jett laughed at him. Lane was happy for both his friends for finding such understanding and giving women that they clearly adored. Two years ago, Jett and Ryker both being out of the military and married or engaged to wonderful women was not something Lane could have believed would happen. Now, here they were, and he was the one alone.

It had been Sarah back home that had gotten him through the worst days during his years in the military. Since the first time they met during freshman year of high school, she had been his everything. Not once had he ever imagined that just as he retired and returned home she would be gone and he would be forced to raise his daughter without her, yet that was the reality that one god awful act of nature had generated.

Twenty month old Sophie was his salvation. Her smiling face had pulled him kicking and screaming back from the edge when the tornado had decimated his future. Even on the worst of days when he walked into her daycare, as soon as she caught sight and launched her tiny body at him, he would find himself smiling despite the pain. It was getting easier to once again taste food, to hear birds singing, to enjoy the small things. He had even started planning small trips with Sophie. Shaking his head, he pulled himself back to the subject on the table.

"I'll call Ryker this evening," Lane stated checking his watch. "I have to go pick up Sophie shortly."

"You want me to throw a couple extra steaks on the grill tonight?" Jett asked as he stood to exit.

Jett often had him over for dinner. It was just one of the ways he tried to make Lane's load a little lighter, and it was appreciated more than he could ever had put into words.

"Nah, I think we will just do mac and cheese with the three hundredth showing of Finding Nemo for entertainment. Make it an early night with just me and my favorite girl."

"Okay," Jett said rising. "See you in the morning."

Lane raised a hand in dismissal and turned back to his work. His eyes caught the invitation on the corner of his desk. Picking it up, he read: *"You are cordially invited to the one-year memorial celebration..."* his eyes shifted to Sarah's picture on the front of his desk facing him.

In two weeks, it would be one year since the day that had hurtled his life down a road he didn't recognize. One year since he had kissed his darling wife good-bye as she headed off to work, never knowing it was the end of their journey together. One year and he still didn't understand why she had to be the one to go, but acceptance was dawning little by little. He was finally able to talk about her, about the good times. He was doing the best he could, and was blessed with friends that helped to make it just a bit easier.

"One year, sweetheart. We made it a year," he whispered running a finger down the glass covering her face.

Inhaling, he closed his computer and headed for the door. His daughter was waiting and she didn't care if he was having a rough day or not. She expected his smiling face to walk into that daycare in a few minutes. Sarah would have adored the toddler, Lane thought as he conjured a picture of the little chattering box of happiness in his head. He was grateful she had been so young when her mother passed that she didn't have to carry that sadness. He had made it one year because of the gift Sarah had left behind. For that reason he carried on, and each day the good memories they continued to make had begun to overshadow the dark cloud in the rearview mirror.

*****

Sydney pulled into the driveway, and grabbing the bag on the passenger side seat headed for the front door. It was a familiar routine. Even though it wasn't her home, she was there so often it had become a comfortable environment for her. She loved getting to see Sophie so often, and she tried to lighten Lane's load of responsibility whenever possible. Sophie was growing so fast it was hard to keep her in clothes and shoes that fit. Sydney smiled to herself as she remembered the ugly deep purple shoes, three sizes too small that Lane had bought for the little girl when she had mentioned her needing new ones. Sydney had gently waved off his embarrassment and offered to return them and find another pair. Sophie would love the sparkly pink ballet slipper style shoes she was carrying in the brightly colored bag.

Ringing the doorbell, Sydney waited for Lane to come to the door. She turned to gaze absently around, listening for signs that someone was at home. While Lane was always alone and didn't seem to mind her intrusion, she didn't want to overstep her welcome. She could hear noises indicating two sets of feet headed her direction.

"Hey," Lane said swinging the door open with a smile, "Did I forget you were coming over?"

"I don't know. Did you?" she teased.

"Nee… Nee… Nee..." A tiny body propelled at her as she deftly reached down and hoisted Sophie up into her arms.

"How is my sweet girl today?" she said nuzzling the little neck, and being rewarded with a giggle as Sophie tried to wiggle away from the invading fingers she poked into the chunky belly.

"Guess what I got for you today?" she directed the question at the little girl, who gifted her with an excited clap.

"Babeee?" she asked wiggling around excitedly.

Dolls were definitely Sophie's favorite toy option these days, but that also meant everyone from grandparents to godparents and friends went overboard on loading her up on them. Sydney would guess the tiny tyke already owned forty dolls of various shapes and sizes.

"No," Sydney put her down a few feet inside the front door as Lane closed the door behind her. Digging around dramatically in the bag, she pulled out a shoe like it was a magician's rabbit. She was rewarded with a big gasp, as Sophie immediately clutched the shoes to her chest as if they were the best present she had received in her short life.

"You are spoiling her," Lane said with no heat behind the statement.

She tilted her head up at him and gave him a saucy look.

"*You* can't be trusted with purchasing shoes, and in this case she needed new ones. She is growing like a weed," she said in a sing song tone poking Sophie in the belly again. She was rewarded with another giggle, before the little girl plopped down on the floor and attempted to put a new shoe on by herself.

"That she is, and you are right about her needing new shoes. They were a bit tight this morning when I put her old ones on. I will repay you as I'm certain those were much more expensive than the ones you were returning," he started into the room.

"Lane, don't worry about it…my treat."

He had a strained look on his face when he turned back that immediately had her worried, uncertain of what he was about to say.

"What is that look for?" she asked bluntly, pointing a finger at his face.

"It's just... I have this gigantic favor to ask of Clementine and you. I feel bad doing so right after you," he waved a hand down toward the shoe that Sophie was still fussing with.

"Lane, it's what friends do. What's up?"

"Well, we got the protection detail at the conference in Dallas...," he said with a big grin.

"That is fabulous!" She caught herself moving forward to hug him, but stopped mid-stride. It was a line they never crossed. She hugged her friends, but Lane just never struck her as someone who would appreciate the affection.

"Yes, but we have to go next week for six days straight," he continued with a small grimace.

"Oh, wow! That *is* bad timing."

His head cocked to one side, "Why?"

"Clementine is already a bit," she made crazy hands in the vicinity of her head, "over not having enough time with Jett to just sit and plan the wedding."

"What is left? They have dresses, tuxes, cake, location and each other."

She laughed out loud at his statement.

"Thank you! I said the exact same thing, but Clementine didn't seem to appreciate my *approach* to wedding planning."

"Good to know, I will definitely avoid that pitfall. Maybe we could make this work for us. If we go all week, and then you, Clementine and Darby came to Dallas for a fun weekend totally on me! We could spend some time just giving her undivided attention. I could even ask my mom to come down after work on Friday to get Sophie for the weekend. She only works four hours on Fridays, so she could get here before you were ready to leave."

Sydney thought about the plan for a second thinking through the details in her mind.

"That might just work and solve several problems at once. As for Sophie, no worries. We'd love to have her for the week."

"This is day and night with a toddler," he warned.

She turned to him, "You don't think we can do it?"

He raised his hands in mock surrender with a big grin, "I'm not crazy! I am just going to say thank you and leave it at that."

She glanced down at her watch.

"Well, I have to run. Fletcher and I have dinner plans in thirty minutes."

"How is our boy Fletcher treating you?" Lane asked seeming to truly be interested.

"Great! He's a good guy, and we are at a good place. I know we aren't all lovey-dovey like Jett and Clementine or Ryker and Darby…"

"Hey, you will get no judgement from me," he said. "If he makes you happy and you can't imagine yourself with anyone else, then hell with the rest of us and our opinions."

"Thanks," she said leaning down to give Sophie a hug and finish putting on shoe number two.

Her brain wandered away, digesting Lane's words. Did Fletcher make her happy? True, she was grateful to finally have someone to spend time with, and he did little things she found endearing. As she stole a glance up at the man leaning against the wall opposite her, she felt a little flutter of doubt skitter through her mind. As for being the only person she could imagine herself with… that was a lot more complicated.

Fletcher wasn't warm and openly prone to public displays of affection such as those Lane gave Sophie, Jett lathered on Clementine or Ryker on Darby. With that much palpable love and attentiveness flowing all around her, she sometimes found herself mentally willing Fletcher to just take her hand during a show, or give her a peck on the cheek for no good reason. In almost nine months of dating, it hadn't happened once. A chaste kiss at the front door over time had become a bit more aggressive, but he didn't seem inclined to take it further, which seemed odd to her.

"Talk to me," Lane said quietly.

"What?" She brought her thoughts back to the present.

"You have that look, like you need to know something but aren't sure how to ask?"

She hesitated.

"Ask!"

She studied her hands as she said, "How long before you think two adults should," she turned toward Sophie who was engaged in trying on shoes, "Sleep together?" She lowered her voice to a whisper.

"Wow! Okay, maybe I'm not the best person..."

"You're a guy. I need a guy's perspective," she mumbled as her old insecurities rose to the surface.

"I have very, very limited knowledge in this area...Sarah was the only woman... and I'm not certain... okay..."

She looked up at him waiting. She could have sworn the man was blushing under his deep tan.

"How long you should wait should be a discussion you and Fletcher have. But *wanting* to... *that* should be there almost from the get go. Friendship, respect and all that have to be ingredients in a great relationship... but if you don't have the fire? What fun is there in that?" he asked as his dimples came out to mirror his huge grin.

"I think I'm broken," Sydney said suddenly before she could think better of the comment.

He laughed out loud, and then must have seen the horror she felt and bit down on his lip halting any further mirth.

"Syd, there is nothing wrong with you. Tell me this, have you ever caught yourself staring at Fletcher's mouth praying he would kiss you?" he asked moving away from the wall. "Have you felt your heart stop when you catch him looking at you for no apparent reason? Have you ever just had to reach out and touch him for no good reason other than absorbing his heat?"

Sydney swallowed harshly around the warmth coursing through her body at Lane's words. She wanted to cry because she would answer "no" to each of those questions. She wanted to hold Fletcher's hand just because she wanted to feel *something*. But the feelings Lane was describing made her realize she had made a huge mistake asking him such a question. She needed to give her relationship time to percolate… perhaps these things would come, she reasoned.

She glanced at her watch, "Thanks for the insight Lane, but I really have to run. Bye, sweetie," she said back to Sophie. Pulling the door open, she all but ran for her car.

She was definitely going to pay more attention tonight, maybe she wasn't broken… maybe she was just distracted. She could hope!

CHAPTER 2

Lane looked down at the phone as he laid it on the table and slid into the bar chair at the table Ryker and Jett already occupied. He hoped everything was okay with Sophie back home, but he was semi-concerned that Sydney wouldn't tell him if there was a problem for fear that he would go rushing away from the job and to his daughter's side, which he would! Her tone tonight was a bit off, and it had him on edge.

"What's with the look?" Ryker groused at him, drawing his eyes up and away from the phone in confusion.

"Huh?"

"You look like someone with the weight of the world on his shoulders," Jett interjected.

"Syd, just seemed off…"

"You think it's something with Sophie?"

"I don't think so," he hesitated mulling the conversation over in his mind, "Because I talked to Sophie, and besides not understanding what she was saying, she chattered away happily at me."

Jett shrugged, "So don't worry about it?"

"Yeah," he mumbled picking up the menu.

It had been a great week and the women would all be coming to join them late the next night. He would be able to tell at that point if something was wrong with Sydney. He was suddenly concerned that the conversation they had last week about Fletcher might have hit a nerve causing a change in their relationship, and that was accounting for her hesitation tonight.

"I appreciate you dragging yourself away from Tyler and Darby this week, and giving us a hand," Lane turned toward Ryker.

"No, problem. I like to keep the skills fresh, get off the farm and stretch my legs," Ryker said without hesitation.

"You already tired of married life?" Jett teased.

"Hell no! I love Darby, but I'm still adjusting to the softer and more emotional ticks of having a woman around all the time," he said with a curious look on his face. "It's a skill I am having to learn quickly."

Lane laughed at him, "Yeah, I remember that first year of marriage. I was so grateful when I got deployed, and I could breathe without being worried she was going to start crying," he felt his heart constrict. What he wouldn't give to have Sarah underfoot now. He needed to talk about her and recall the memories, even those that hadn't seemed good at the time, were bittersweet, stinging a little still, but healing along with the pain.

"Darby told me the memorial service is next week," Ryker ventured.

"Yeah, it's a big deal for her family, but it still seems unreal," Lane looked off past both of those seated.

"You and stories of Sarah got us all through some dark times. I just never thought..." Jett caught himself.

"I know. I always thought Bryce would be the worst thing we all had to live through," Ryker said.

"Definitely sucks losing both of them. I feel lost sometimes, but I have Sophie. Each day gets a bit easier, but I still miss both of them more than I ever thought possible. I am so grateful to both of you, and Clementine and Sydney. I couldn't have made it this far with my sanity intact without you all."

"You would have done the same for us," Jett said.

"You did the same for me... kicking my butt about Darby when I was so worried about what Bryce would have thought," Ryker said.

"How did we get so far off topic?"

"I don't know, but I do appreciate the opportunity this week," Ryker said unequivocally.

Lane picked up the menu. These two men, more like brothers than coworkers, were such a big part of his life, and he truly could never imagine what he would do without them. He never had to hide his feelings, or filter his speech with them.

"So the women will all be here tomorrow, and I know we need to let Clementine corral us all for a bit of wedding planning. Any other ideas on what we should do from there?"

Lane saw a look pass between Jett and Ryker, before they both turned back his direction.

"I'm not going to like this am I?"

"What are your thoughts on entertaining Sydney on your own Saturday afternoon? If you aren't comfortable, just say so, but we thought maybe..."

So they didn't each need a third wheel for a romantic date in the city, he got the message loud and clear. They had done so much for him he could take one for the team. Besides, he didn't mind spending time with Sydney. They got along great and she was not fussy like some women he had met. Although, without Sophie

A SOLDIER'S VOW -- 32

around, it would be the first time it was just the two of them together, and he hoped they would find things to talk about. Even if things were odd between them, it was a small price to pay for everything Ryker and Jett had done for him.

*****

"I think that is it," Clementine announced excitedly, closing the binder she had been making notes in during breakfast.

"Thank goodness," Jett said leaning over to buffer his response by kissing his future bride.

Sydney finished making a few notes in the notebook she always had stowed in her purse. As the Maid of Honor, she felt obligated to ensure that all the details were seen to in order to ensure the day was perfect. The more she took on, the less Clementine had to worry her sick about.

"You need to eat something," Lane said bumping her shoulder. "You've been so busy taking notes that you haven't touched your breakfast."

She turned quickly to find him in her personal space bubble, "Thank you, daddy," she quipped at him with a sarcastic grin.

"Don't complain to me when you are hungry in a little while," he said arching an eyebrow her direction.

She rolled her eyes immaturely at him, but took a bit of the omelet anyway. It was delicious, and she discovered that she was hungry. Closing the notebook, she dug in, listening to the conversation going on around her.

"So Sophie didn't give you any major trouble?" Lane asked in a hushed tone.

"Are you kidding? The child adores Syd and all she has to do is give her a look," Clementine cut in before Sydney could answer. "And Syd has the patience of Job with her, even let her sleep with her several nights."

Sydney looked up and gave Clementine a warning look.

She turned to Lane to explain, and found he had an eyebrow quirked at her again.

"She didn't sleep with me *every* night," she said evasively. Not adding that one night she had gotten there too late and Clementine already had Sophie tucked up in her own little bed.

"It's all good. That's probably my fault. She sleeps with me most nights," he shrugged not seeming apologetic at all about the bad habit.

"So how do you deal with the flopping arms?" she asked with a grin.

"Oh my god, seriously? I wake up with her across my chest, her feet in my nose and once when she socked me in the middle of the night I thought I was going to have a black eye," he laughed with Sydney over that little tidbit.

"Any who..." Jett broke in drawing their attention back to the center of the table. "Now that we have all the wedding details sorted out, we thought we could spend the afternoon site seeing and..." he looked at Lane with a small bob of his neck.

Sydney knew it was a signal of sorts.

"What's up?" she asked turning to Lane.

"Ryker and Jett would like to spend the day with their respective wife and wife to be... alone," he said glaring across the table at Jett.

"Oh. I'm sorry. I don't mean to be a third wheel...," Sydney felt out of place suddenly. Of course the married and engaged couples would desire to spend some time alone together.

"Hey," Lane said reaching out and laying his hand on her arm. "I invited you as a thank you for taking care of Sophie. Screw them... we are going to have some fun!"

"You don't have to...," she felt her blood pressure spike. She never spent time alone with Lane or any man other than Fletcher for that matter in the past several years. She felt gawky and unsure of herself and worried that she would say or do something to jeopardize Lane and her easygoing friendship.

"I'm okay with you coming along to the spa," Clementine said punching Jett.

"Absolutely," Darby joined in.

"No! You all deserve downtime together... go... have fun... I'm sure Lane and I can find something to do," forcibly plastering a smile on her face to throw them off her discomfort.

She turned to Lane for reinforcements.

"What did you have in mind for the day?"

"Well, there is the water park...," Lane offered up.

She wrinkled her nose.

"Skydiving."

She gave him a get serious look.

"Hiking and picnic lunch?"

"That could work," she agreed perking up. The thought of hiking in the fresh open air and picnicking was more appealing than even the spa in her book.

"I realize you might want to go to the spa...," Lane said hesitantly.

"No, seriously this could be fun. Besides they really do need some alone time," she whispered conspiratorially at him.

"Agreed. If I'd known, though, I would have had you bring Fletcher."

She felt the tension tighten her shoulders. After the argument she'd had a few nights before with Fletcher, it was obvious they differed on several key areas. He had given her an ultimatum of sorts, and she needed some time away to evaluate her options. Some wide open spaces and time to ruminate was just what the doctor ordered.

"I'm good," she said taking another bite.

"Okay, then. I'm going to run and get a few picnic items. Want to meet me down here in say," he glanced at his watch, "thirty minutes?"

She nodded up at him.

A hand on her other arm had her swiveling around to the worried eyes of Clementine and Darby beyond her.

"I'm sorry. We didn't mean to abandon you."

"Cleo, Darby… seriously, Lane and I get on fine, and an afternoon hiking in the fresh air sounds great."

She realized when she turned back to finish her breakfast, she truly meant it. Not feeling the least bit slighted, she also wasn't about to read anything into the bubbly feeling in her chest. She just hoped she didn't do anything to make Lane regret this decision.

*****

Lane lathered his hair, singing as he went about his tasks. He had just enough time to finish cleaning the busy day off and get downstairs before dinner. Jett had already taken a shower and headed down before he jumped in, so he had the room to himself and was grateful not to have to turn down the singing volume.

It had been a relaxing and fun day, and an evening out just with adults seemed like the perfect conclusion to the weekend. They would all be headed back to the real world in the morning, but tonight they were all cutting loose. Clementine had even talked them in to bringing nice clothes, which for him basically entailed a dress shirt and black jeans. Clementine's schemes normally made him a bit on edge, but this one time he felt like rejoining the adult world and just enjoying himself.

He was starving, so as long as food was served wherever they were headed, he was game for anything they could throw at him. Sydney and he had hiked for a good six hours, stopping when they found the perfect deserted place for lunch. It had been a wonderful laid back afternoon exploring, talking and absorbing the great outdoors. He had been pleasantly surprised at how much fun she was to hang out with when none of the other friends or Sophie was around to steal her limelight. He could totally understand what Fletcher saw in her and why he liked having her one on one rather than in a crowd. Lane might not like the guy personally, he was just a bit too reserved and full of himself for Lane's tastes, but he had won the jackpot in Sydney.

After Sarah's death, Sydney more than anyone else had pitched in to help with all the little things Sophie and he needed. A fussy unhappy baby who constantly cried for her momma and a recent widower were not a hell of a lot of fun and yet not once had she ever complained. Now a year later, he could honestly say that while Jett and Ryker were moving on to the next stage of their lives he found that Sydney being single and hanging out with him and Sophie made things easier.

More than once during the day he had considered asking her to accompany him the following weekend to the memorial service. He could use the support and had instinctively known she would understand and graciously lend a shoulder. But he hadn't broached the subject, not certain how the invitation would be received. Besides, he had reasoned, it was entirely possible she had already asked Fletcher.

Jumping out of the shower, he checked his watch and realized he had been lollygagging longer than he had intended. His short hair needed only a towel and a pea sized mound of gel to be considered styled. His clothes were in place with a few decisive moves and he was headed for the door in short order. He didn't like being late, no matter how informal the situation, so he had honed a routine that allowed him shower to door in ten minutes or less.

Taking the stairs, he was on the ground floor and walking into the lobby area where a good-sized crowd had gathered for happy hour. Spotting Jett above the

Angelica Kate -- 39

crowd, he acknowledged him with a slight nod and started weaving his way into the horde. While making a few apologies, he tried to maneuver his considerable frame through the tight lanes of bodies dotting the entire distance to his group of friends.

"Hey there." A blonde he didn't recognize stopped his progress, giving him a huge smile. She was almost as tall as his six foot frame in her spiky sandals. He quickly assessed her slim figure, manicured hands, wide-swath of dangly shiny jewelry on her neck, ears and wrists and immaculately applied heavy make-up. Besides that and the overwhelming amount of perfume she had bathed in, nothing else of importance registered with him. He assumed she wasn't talking to him and continued walking.

A hand snaking over his arm stopped him mid stride. "I'm Cynthia," the same blonde said holding her hand out in greeting.

He was confused, did he know her? Why was she being so forward?

"Lane," he said, taking her hand out of politeness. "Do I know you?"

"No, but I'm hoping by the end of the night we are *much* better acquainted." For the first time it registered that she was flirting with him, something that no one had attempted in quite a number of years. He kept his polite face on as the shock of the situation fully registered.

"Listen, I'm not being rude but I'm meeting friends," he pointed across the room.

"Maybe I could join you," she purred, coming up close to his ear. She purposely blew on the lobe, which he assumed was meant as a come on but made him want to shudder and run.

The woman was a pariah and much too forward for his taste. And that was if he was even in the market for a new companion or wife, which he wasn't. He caught site of Clementine on Jett's arm and Darby with Ryker's arm around her, and recognized that such a woman would never hold a candle to either of them. They were stunning to look at and loved completely. They hadn't needed flashy jewelry, perfume or aggressive personalities to harpoon men. That was what Sarah and he had possessed, and in order to ever tempt him again, a woman would need to get that and not employ heavy-handed tactics to ensnare him.

"I'm sorry," he said trying to step away and unwind her arm.

"We could be great together," she said in the same slow purr and winked at him.

How was he to get out of her clutches unscathed and without being completely rude?

"Are you seriously going to keep me waiting for dinner, after all that physical activity this afternoon," Sydney's voice cut in from his right side. He saw the

Angelica Kate -- 41

distaste for the intrusion on Cynthia's face before turning his head to Sydney.

"Who are you?" Cynthia fairly shrieked at Sydney.

"The one he's leaving with," Sydney said giving her the same no-nonsense look she sometimes gave Sophia.

He felt Cynthia's arm slide from his and he was free to follow Sydney. He bit back the smile that threatened to break free.

"You are formidable when you want to be," he bent to whisper in Sydney's ear.

"I don't like her kind," she shrugged. "Besides, Darby gave me tequila and I'm feeling a bit..." she shrugged and grinned up at him. "Feisty. Yeah, that's it. Feisty."

Not once before had he seen this side of Sydney, but he was caught off guard by how much he was enjoying it. The woman was a veritable treasure chest of surprises he thought, following her. She had dressed up for the evening in a simple light blue dress and sandals with only a watch and a pair of tiny silver hoop earrings as adornment. Even in such simplicity, she put Cynthia to shame. Although Sydney often described herself as mousy, she was anything but he thought, indexing her attributes. She had brown hair, yes, but in the light it shimmered with natural highlights of gold and red, and her eyes always revealed her emotions when she spoke. She was straight forward, smart as a whip and had a wicked sense of humor, which had been showcased by that little scene she caused. He couldn't help but find his admiration for her jump a notch.

"Seriously, we had to send a girl to rescue you?" Jett sent him a disbelieving look, attached to the sarcastic gibe when they finally met up with the group.

"Hey! I am a *woman* thank you very much," Sydney corrected Jett.

That's a fact. The happy mood that had been with him all day wasn't going anywhere soon, Lane realized with a start.

CHAPTER 3

"What are you going to have Sophie wear?" Sydney asked Clementine as she came out of the dressing room.

"Lane is coming with Jett for their tuxedo fittings and I asked that they bring Sophie so I could have her try on a couple of the little flower girl dresses they have here," Clementine said glancing down at her cell phone.

Sydney stood in her bare feet, tugging at the dress she had on, trying to keep the distaste from showing on her face. Unlike the one she had just discarded, this one was long and she thought the color and fit made her look frumpy and washed out. But, it was Clementine's day, so if she wanted her to wear sack cloth, then she would with a smile.

"You really don't like that one do you?" Clementine pressed, moving her head from examining the dress to Sydney's face.

"Clem, we have been going back and forth for weeks. You need to just pick one so we can get them sized. We have less than seven weeks now and I promise I will wear whatever you want me to. This is your day!"

"But you don't love it," Clementine whined.

"Honey, it's your wedding, I would go naked if you asked."

"Whoa," Jett said coming through the open doorway in time to catch that statement. "No upstaging my bride," he plopped a kiss on Clementine's upturned face.

"I think it would be more like making all the guests ill," Sydney quipped.

"Syd, turn around one more time," Clementine said doing circles with her finger in the air to demonstrate.

She did as instructed, and then stood waiting for the next set of instructions from the bride.

"Nee... Nee," Sophie screamed, entering the little mirrored area in Lane's arms. The little girl maneuvered

A SOLDIER'S VOW -- 46

out of her father's arm and was at Sydney's feet in short order.

She bent down with a smile, "Do you like my dress?"

The little girl made a weird motion with her head, wrinkling her little nose. Sydney bit down on her lip. *Out of the mouths of babes!*

"That's what I thought," Clementine said, "Something about it just doesn't do you justice."

"Can I change now?" Sydney asked, uncomfortable being the center of attention.

"Could you try on the other one, just one more time?" Clementine made a prayer or begging motion, Sydney wasn't sure which with her hands mirrored by her eyes.

Sydney nodded, rolling her eyes at Lane as she turned. He in turn bit his lip trying not to laugh. Sophie grabbed her hand as she walked back to the dressing room, obviously intent on following her in to the room beyond.

"Sweetie, let Syd get changed…" Lane tried to redirect the toddler.

"She's okay," Sydney said. "Besides, we are going to try on flower girl dresses. Clementine you want to grab the ones you want her to try on and join us?"

Clementine jumped up, "Yep, and guys, they have someone right next door in the men's dressing area to help with tuxedos."

"You sure she's not too much trouble?" Lane called out.

Sydney shot him a look over her shoulder intended to silence him, and continued to the dressing room.

Fifteen minutes of wrangling Sophie in and out of three dresses, before Clementine chose the one she liked, had Sydney all but worn out. She wiggled into the other bridesmaid dress one last time. It was a bit too small, but they had been assured Clementine a new one could be made in plenty of time for the wedding if they ordered today. Without thinking, Sydney stepped out of the dressing room to hand the toddler back to Lane.

"Zook Da," Sophie said spinning around gleefully.

"You look beautiful," he said crouching down to hold her hand so the twirling didn't upend her.

Sydney was turning away, when she caught Lane's eyes in the mirror.

"What?" She asked suspiciously turning back his direction.

"You aren't zipped up." he said, although something else seemed wrong from the slight coloring around his neck.

"I can't breathe in this, it's too small," she said under her breath, turning slightly so the opening in the back wasn't in his direct line of sight.

"I can see that…"

She almost laughed at the look of pure horror in his eyes.

"Lane, there is no one but us in the store, are you normally this appalled by women's under things, or just mine?" she found the question spilling out before she could suppress the thought.

"I… uh…"

"Are you okay?" She noticed his eyes looked strange, as if something was eating at him. Then suddenly she realized that her legs were bare, and she sucked in a shaky breath. "I… I forgot… the scar…"

Lane looked confused for a moment. Then his eyes drifted down her leg, finding the faded white line.

"I didn't even notice the scar," he said quietly.

She didn't believe him. What else could it have been? The jagged white line that ran from mid-thigh to just below her knee was a stark reminder of those terrifying days when she had been held captive in a dark, musty shack in Peru. If he hadn't come to her rescue when he did, she would have lost the leg. An ugly scar had been a small price to pay. Turning before he could say anything to hurt her fragile pride, she plastered a smile on her face and held her hand out to Sophie.

"Come on, sweetie, let's get out of these dresses," she said as Sophie ran ahead back to the dressing room.

"Sydney!"

She was brought up short by a warm body coming up directly behind her, and a hand placed on her hip to handicap her progress out of the area.

"I never even noticed the scar," Lane repeated quietly, his lips brushing her neck just below her ear, causing tiny shivers to run down her nerve endings. "I was too busy admiring... other things."

As quick as it started the moment ended, and inhaling sharply, she briskly walked toward the dressing room.

Focusing on getting Sophie out of the confection she wore and back into her daily clothes did absolutely nothing to calm her jangled nerves. When she let the little girl out of the dressing room, and assured she was back in the safe arms of her father she sagged against the wall of the tiny space

Good god get it together, Sydney, she chastised herself. *This is Lane we are talking about. The man is perpetually married to his dead wife*. The big brooding, tattooed, ex-military single father was completely off limits for her. She had known that from the day he had pulled her out of that hellhole, even though his was the face she so often saw in her dreams. His was the face that ended her nightmares and replaced them with a sense of safety and peace.

She had been able to hide her feelings through the long months as she tried to convince her heart that what she felt was simply gratitude and hero worship for what he had done for her. None of the reasoning helped to calm her revved up body and the confused longing one small peck on the neck had produced.

This was bad, so bad! She had to pull it together. She couldn't be attracted to Lane. They were friends. That was all. Squaring her shoulders she decided to put the inconsequential episode out of her mind, and focus on something less fanciful. She knew Lane was being kind, and just because she had such a knee jerk reaction, it didn't prove that he had meant anything by it. She remembered the woman in Dallas, and with a final shudder, her brain talked her body into remembering that Lane could have any woman he wanted. He certainly wasn't going to fall for one that looked like her.

Pep talk over!

She forced the episode out of her mind, finished changing out of the dress and went in search of Clementine.

*****

The memorial service the previous Saturday had been the only thing Lane could focus on over the course of the day, until that lapse of judgement in the bridal shop. It had been a year, and Saturday had been a time to remember and honor those that had been lost. The size of the hole in his life had never been more evident as he sat amongst the other family members of the 21 people that had died that day. So many tears as fresh as the day the tornado ripped their loved ones away, and yet he had felt a sense of peace.

He and Sarah had talked openly about death during their marriage. Having an active military member in the household had made such conversations necessary. She had known that he put his life on the line every day, so they had discussed it and agreed to treasure every moment they had together, never allowing fear to hinder their plans. They each had agreed to pick themselves up and bully on should something happen to the other one. Of course, they had always believed that Sarah would be the one who needed to move on as his line of work had upped the odds of him being the one to die young. With that situation now reversed, however, he knew that Sarah would expect the same of him. Somewhere she was looking down on him, and waiting for him to take a step forward and quit the holding pattern he had found himself in since that day.

So Saturday, he hadn't put Sophie through the services but instead had left her with Sydney while he went to celebrate Sarah's life and remember for a while. He had stopped by Sarah's grave on the way home, and in that quiet moment asked that she give him the strength to start moving ahead with his life, to make each day the best he could for Sophie, who didn't deserve to be shortchanged because of his unhappiness or Sarah's absence in their lives. And most of all, he told her as he often did how much he loved and missed her.

He hadn't expected some major declaration from beyond, but when he had walked into that shop, his world had shifted. The friend who had helped him through his wife's death cherished Sophie as if she was her own and made each day easier for him had in a moment become something else. He truly hoped it wasn't some sick trick the universe was playing, because until that brain fart, he had never considered that moving on would involve a woman. Being a single father, raising Sophie happy and healthy with the help of his buddies, their wives and Sydney was the plan. It was working.

So why the hell had the sight of her in that splashy little dress caused him to lose his grip on reality? The urge to reach out and run his finger down that exposed back had almost overcome his good senses. And her legs... In the end, he had laid his hand on her hip and whispered in her ear a decidedly intimate comment. He

Angelica Kate -- 53

hadn't been able to forcibly hold back upon seeing the hurt on her face when she thought she had repulsed him. The inhalation of everything Sydney and her leaning back into him for a split second caused the world to stop just long enough for EVERYTHING to change.

He decided that it had to be an aberration from the additional stresses all the reminiscing had loaded up on him. It had gotten him thinking, though, that maybe it was time for him to start dating, for lack of a better word. Just get out of the house for adult time to help with the stresses of raising a toddler, helming a new business and all the other details of his life. He believed in his heart that Sarah would understand, but maybe he needed a bit of advice. Just another perspective might help. Pulling his cell out of his pocket, he dialed Jett.

After a brief conversation Jett hadn't hesitated when Lane asked if he could stop over to discuss something this evening. Lane went inside to grab a couple beers, and quickly check to ensure Sophie was sound asleep in her bed. He was sitting on the deck staring off when Jett rounded the corner less than ten minutes later.

"Hey," Jett's greeting brought Lane out of his stupor.

"Hi. Beer?" Lane extended a bottle his direction.

"When have I ever turned down a cold one?" Jett took the offering and sat down in the chair on the opposite side of Lane.

"Thanks for coming, but if you make fun of me, I will kick your ass."

"Right! Last sparring match you won was... oh yeah, never!" Jett chuckled. "But seriously... what's up?"

Lane inhaled and then just laid it out there, "Do you think it's too early for me to be dating?"

Jett spit beer across the open space in front of him. "Um... wow, where did that come from?"

"I've just been thinking. I miss having someone around, and I kind of promised Sarah I would... you know... move on... if something happened. I just don't know... how soon is too soon?"

"Wow! Maybe you need to talk to Sydney or Clementine... women are so much..."

"No! Definitely not!" Lane didn't think having any conversation of a personal nature with Sydney at the moment was a sensible idea. But this particular one especially was absolutely never going to happen!

"Okay. Then I will tell you my honest thoughts," Lane watched Jett swallow hard. "Only *you* know if it's too soon. Sarah's not coming back, and knowing her as I do and how much she loved both you and Sophie I agree she would want whatever is best for the two of you. How long have you been thinking about this?"

"Since this afternoon," Lane admitted. "I had a situation come up today... with someone who is completely inappropriate..."

"Inappropriate... like a sixteen year old high school girl inappropriate?" Jett asked turning worried eyes his direction.

'NO! Just someone that I shouldn't... well, can't... it just got me thinking that maybe going out... meeting new people and blowing off steam. It might provide a break from business, and everything else I do on a daily basis. I met Sarah my freshman year of high school, and she is the only woman I've ever dated or been with so this is... all new territory for me."

"What do you have to lose? If it's a bust, go back to not dating and give it some more time before you try again," Jett shrugged.

Lane nodded and studied his drink for a few minutes before speaking again.

"So my next question is how would I meet someone? That woman in Dallas was a bit too forward and caused me to think I'm not certain a bar would be..."

"Clementine has lots of friends... and might have some good ideas. Unless this is a secret?"

"Really? In our group, what was the last secret we successfully kept?" He quirked a brow at Jett and waited.

"Point taken. Let me ask her and see what she recommends. Maybe we could even double a time or two, take the stress of the initial meeting off a bit."

"Sounds good."

"Now, about this inappropriate situation..."

"Drop it..." Lane growled.

Jett's hearty laughter was the only response, further irritating his conscience.

*****

The following morning as Sydney walked her first client of the day to the door, she glanced at Clementine sitting on the arm of a chair in the lobby. She could almost feel the excitement roiling off her, but she focused first on getting her client out the door. Turning, she arched her brow at Clementine and just waited for a moment.

"Spill!" she ordered when Clementine didn't volunteer a single word.

"Oh my goodness, Jett just told me the craaaazzziiiest thing ever!" She exclaimed flailing her arms around for effect.

"I do think that might be an exaggeration but...?" Sydney waved her hand for Clementine to continue her story.

"Lane is dating again!"

Sydney felt her stomach hit the ground as every last particle of air exited her lungs. She reached out to the nearest chair and sank into it. Shaking her head, she focused on Clementine.

"How long has this been going on?"

Obviously if he had a girlfriend she had completely misunderstood that moment yesterday outside the dressing room. She felt bereft. A miserable sense of dread settled over her. *Of course he would start dating sometime.* And it stood to reason that someone as perfect as he was wouldn't be interested in someone like her, but still, she had for a moment... she stopped the thought before it fully formed! Swallowing hard, she attempted to focus on the words coming out of Clementine's lips.

"He just talked to Jett about it last night," Clementine was gushing.

"So who is she?"

"No one yet. Didn't you hear me?" Clementine cocked her head at Sydney like she was daft.

"You caught me off guard, start from the beginning."

"He told Jett that he wanted to start dating, getting to know women and have some fun away from the business and Sophie. Since he only has ever dated Sarah and it's been over a year, he was asking for advice last night."

"That's a little different from *Lane is dating again*."

"How?" Clementine looked at her with a confused expression.

"Never mind," Sydney didn't want to get into a semantics discussion.

"So, Jett and I are going to double date with him to get him started, and I agreed to see if one of my single friends might be a good match."

"Oh no, matchmaking can be a tricky business. If they hit it off, great, but if something goes south… there goes your friendship and all the blame comes your direction for the relationship tanking," Sydney hoped that she could dissuade Clementine from her path.

"So, we make sure I don't set him up with my really good friends, like you for example. We need to find him someone that isn't so close but is still really great. I was thinking Tracy," Clementine continued obviously not going to be deterred from her course of action.

Sydney rolled her eyes.

"I know you didn't get along with her, but she is hot."

"And she knows it and is mean to those of us who aren't. Besides she's a bit of a B-I-T-C-H," Sydney spelled out the word for emphasis.

"Yeah, and Lane is a sweetie." Clementine chewed on her lip, thinking. "Then, how about Nina?"

"She is smart and super nice but HATES kids, remember?"

"That's right… the debate in sophomore English. Who hates kids?" Clementine asked with puzzlement on her face.

"I think we discussed that at length when it happened. Remember?"

"I forgot in my excitement, and Sophie would probably appreciate someone who likes little people. Especially if they get serious," she sat thinking for a minute. "What about Grace?"

"Clementine, she has already accepted a teaching position in China this fall for three years."

Sydney was perplexed at how nonchalant Clementine was being about the whole subject. This was Lane after all. He deserved the perfect candidate not just the first one pulled out of her address book.

"How about Meghan?" Clementine bullied on, not deterred by Sydney's truth bombs about her previous selections.

Sydney stopped and pondered that one. Meghan was a new friend to their circle and worked as a therapist with military veterans in a reintegration program in the city. She was also working towards partner in Dr. Bershaw's practice, which is where they had all met. Meghan was a few inches taller than Sydney, dishwater blonde, an avid runner, beautiful in a classic manner and always happy. There was nothing she could think of that could legitimately disqualify her.

"Well, she would be the best out of all the ones you have mentioned," Sydney said plastering a smile on her face.

"Wonderful. I will call and set something up with her. Are you willing to watch Sophie for a night?"

"Sure, just not tomorrow because I already have plans," Sydney said defensively.

"I was thinking Friday. That way none of us have to work the next morning if things go well and it gets late," Clementine waggled her eyebrows so Sydney knew exactly where her mind was going with the suggestion.

"I have the next two Fridays open," she said curtly, turning to go to her office.

A tiny black cloud followed her. If Lane found someone new, their routine would change and access to Sophie would become much more limited leaving a huge void in her life. Until that moment, she hadn't realized how much she looked forward to her time with the toddler, and to be honest, with Lane. She was realistic enough to realize that he would probably remarry someday "down the road when he got over Sarah's death." Now that she was facing that day, it wasn't settling well with her. It also meant clearly that whatever imaginings she had at the dress shop, they were just that, *imaginings*, but the damage had been done. She was questioning her relationship with Fletcher. Not once in their time together had he made her feel a fraction of what a few whispered words from Lane had.

CHAPTER 4

Lane let himself into the house, widening his eyes against the tiredness weighting them. Looking around, he noticed the house had been cleaned up. Sydney had a habit of doing that every time she was over. He grinned. *She just couldn't help herself.*

Walking down the hall, he glanced into Sophie's room. Empty. Continuing down the hall to his own room, he heard the television making white noise sounds. He kept an old VHS player and Disney movies galore on his main dresser. He and Sophie often watched a movie together as he tried to get her settled down for the night.

Swinging the door back he found the object of his search right there in the middle of the big king bed, sound asleep, curled up into the woman arched around her. His heart lurched at the sight.

His baby girl lay, thumb in her mouth dead to the world with a sweet smile on her face. Sydney had her arms around her and was also lightly snoring, telling him she was in a deep slumber. He looked down at his watch and grimaced when he saw the early hour of 2 a.m. reflected back at him. He couldn't wake her he thought, not after drafting her into babysitting so he could go out for the evening. Walking further into the room, stepping softly to ensure they didn't wake, he pulled a throw blanket from a side chair that had been there since Sarah had placed it there when remodeling their room the year before she passed. He carefully draped it over Sydney, noting that Sophie was already curled up with her favorite princess blanket and a baby doll.

He stood for a moment taking in the tender scene. Sydney looked so peaceful in sleep. Glancing around as if someone would catch him, he reached a finger out and hooked the hair falling over her eyes with his forefinger. Drawing the errant curl back so it wasn't covering her face, he took in her make-up and defect free skin. He couldn't resist a feather light trace down her cheek. Realizing she could wake and he wouldn't be able to explain away his actions, he turned from the bed, gathered up the pajama bottoms he usually wore and decided to add a t-shirt since Sydney would be in the house when he woke. Flipping off the television, he took one last look back at the cute twosome and then headed to the bathroom.

Minutes later, hands behind his head as he contemplated sleep on the oversized sofa in the living room, he thought back over his evening. For a first date, it had been nice. Meghan was a therapist, beautiful externally and just as fascinating on the inside. She definitely was a talker, and between her and Clementine, the conversation never lagged for a moment over the course of several hours. She could converse on a host of topics, asked lots of questions, which having dealt with Sydney and Clementine appeared to be a trait therapist all had in common. He could not put his finger on anything that he would change about her.

So why, when she had asked about seeing him again, *just the two of them*, had he hesitated?

He thought back to the first time he saw Sarah and knew without reserve what was missing. There had been no spark. Not even a flicker. Even when Meghan had purposely brushed against him, he had felt nothing. Maybe he had lost the ability to feel... His errant mind flashed to a moment outside a dressing room, and he found himself rubbing his eyes as he recalled that inferno of feelings that had engulfed him. *Apparently he was capable of feeling desire for someone, unavailable as she might be.*

He decided that perhaps a second date with Meghan would be a good idea. At least he would know if there was a chance for them. If not, that would be that. It might come down to the fact he wasn't ready, and he didn't want to waste anyone's time while he tried to figure it out. Decision made, he felt his brain letting go and within a short time he was sound asleep.

He didn't remember another thing until a bundle of giggles jumped on top of him at 6 a.m. the following morning.

*****

Sydney rolled over confused by the light shining in her eyes. When Sophie stirred next to her, her befuddled brain started quickly filling in details. Glancing around she realized that she was still in Lane's bed, but judging from the light coming through the windows, it was morning. She picked up her cellphone. She hadn't missed a call. She couldn't imagine Lane ever not calling if he was going to be out all night, but odder things had happened.

"Nee… nee," Sophie said stretching out.

"Morning, sweet baby," she said leaning down to nuzzle the little girl. *She was about the sweetest thing ever!*

"Juice!" Sophie demanded.

"Yes, little task master," she said with a grin swinging her feet off the bed. She needed a cup of coffee to get her fully in gear. Unfortunately, the toddler didn't require any motivation to start her morning off at a run and was out of the room in a flash.

"Daa..." came from the other room with a giggle followed right behind it.

"How's my baby girl?" Lane's gravely sleep ridden voice could be heard from the living room.

Sydney walked down the hall and stood staring at the prone man on the couch.

"Morning," he said looking up at her.

"Why didn't you wake me?"

"Got in late, and you were already asleep."

"Ah… date went well then?" She tried to keep her tone even.

"Yeah… I guess…" he stood suddenly and came to stop right in front of her for a moment. As she looked up, he looked about ready to say something but then kept walking.

Confused she turned to his back, "We thought you would like Meghan. You seem… I don't know…"

Angelica Kate -- 67

"Coffee?" he asked holding up a package of the brand she kept in her own fridge at home.

"Yes, please! But first I need to use the restroom... did you know your daughter doesn't like toilets?"

He chuckled, "Yeah, and she won't let you go alone. I got one of those big packs of toothbrushes at Sam's Club last month. It's in the drawer to the right of the sink... if you need one."

"Thank you," she said padding down the hall.

"Nee... nee," the little shadow followed.

After twenty minutes of taking care of what normally took only ten without a toddler shadowing her, she walked back into the kitchen.

"Sorry, she is quite attached to you," Lane said handing her a cup of coffee.

"It's all good. I get plenty of peace and quiet at my house."

"You want pancakes?" Lane asked Sophie.

"Mik mee..." she said with a big clap.

Sydney gave Lane a questioning look.

"Mickey Mouse pancakes," he said opening a cabinet and grabbing a bag of miniature chocolate chips. "We went to a restaurant once and they had them with chocolate chips and now... that's how she assumes pancakes are always made."

"And you being the doting dad… make them like Mickey Mouse?"

"What can I say, I'm a sucker for a pretty face." He grinned over at Sophie. "Let Syd help you up into your chair," he said to the wiggly tot.

Sydney took a swig of energy and walked over to help. Handing Sophie a juice cup, she turned back to Lane.

"So tell me what happened last night?"

"Nothing, we had a great time," he said remaining focused on the pancakes.

"She wasn't pretty enough?"

"No, she was beautiful."

"Yup, that she is," Sydney said under her breath.

"Stop it! You are gorgeous…"

"Don't!" she held up her hand to stop his lame next words. "And you got along great?"

"Yes, we had a blast. It was lots of fun… we ate dinner, went to a comedy club…t he evening flew by..." he flipped a pancake onto a plate and handed it to her. She grinned at the perfectly formed pancake with two little ears. "Mikey Mouse it is, I'm impressed."

"You have no idea of all my *secret talents*."

"I'll bet," she snickered. "Oh, wait! You didn't show any of those 'secret talents'" she accentuated the air with italics having put Sophie's plate down in front of her, "to Meghan and she found them lacking… did you?"

Angelica Kate -- 69

"No… we were in public," he reached out and tweaked her side, "Stop it!"

"Hey, I know for a fact you have a ticklish spot…" she challenged back without hesitation.

"Don't you dare…" he turned on her as she ducked and weaved, attempting to get to the spot on his back that was, according to the stories, how Jett and Ryker had on more than one occasion handicapped him to their advantage.

One ninja move later and she was back up against the refrigerator and he had both her hands in one of his, above her head.

"That's not fair," she said, trying to give him her most ferocious glare. A heartbeat later the air was sucked from the room as their eyes met. The entire tone of the interaction went from playful to dangerous with the flick of her tongue over her lips. She watched in fascination as his gaze dropped to her mouth, and his breath caught.

He suddenly released her hands. They dropped like lead weights to her side. She couldn't move and what little air the tiny gasps she could muster provided her lungs wasn't enough. She felt light headed, and when he moved forward a step, she did too. She moved both hands to the front of his shirt. He was so warm through the light material and yet so firm she wanted to explore every muscle, but her hands stayed testing the contact between them that sizzled with electricity she had never experienced first-hand before.

Just when she thought she needed to back away, he did the unthinkable and lowered his dazed eyes back to her lips. Then, his head followed and stopped only a hair's breadth from hers. She looked into his eyes, and the normally light colored lenses were dark and stormy. The sheer wonder of realizing he was just as moved as she was had her rising onto her toes and finishing what he started. For the first breath it was enough to just feel his lips resting on hers, but the low grumble in his throat gave her wings. She moved her head to the right as he went left and completely sealed them together.

She had not ever felt so alive and ready to combust all at the same time. His hand slipped around her and ever so slightly tugged her until she had to move the hands on his chest upward, around his neck and into that short prickly military cut at the back of his head, her breath hitching again as her breasts came to rest flush against him.

This was what every stupid romance movie she had ever seen promised, and yet this was *Lane*. He was one of her best friends, who still mourned his wife and had just started dating another one of her friends. She knew pulling back was the only sane move, and yet as the exploration deepened she knew it was impossible.

DING DONG

Saved by the bell was the first thought that crossed her mind as they jerked apart with a start! Each gaze trained toward the front of the house.

"Nee... neee... bell..." Sophie announced.

Still not able to move or process, she watched as Lane made his way to the front door. His back disappearing around the hallway entrance snapped her out of the fog she was in. Turning, she checked on Sophie and grabbed up her coffee cup.

"Oh my goodness, Sydney," Meghan gasped coming into view. "Lane told me you were his babysitter. It is so good to see you," she gushed coming forward with open arms to give Sydney a hug.

"Wow, Meghan I wasn't expecting you," she said wrapping her arms around the woman not able to look at Lane.

"I just wanted to surprise Lane with a little breakfast from my favorite spot," she said holding up the bakery bag she carried. "We talked about it last night."

"Well, I was just headed out... so you guys have fun," Sydney said, sure her face was going to crack from the effort to keep the smile in place.

She bent down and gave Sophie a kiss on her head, and then without making eye contact with Lane, she grabbed her purse from the chair in the living room and made it to the front door before she felt his hand on her arm.

"I didn't know she was stopping over," he said for her ears alone.

"It was very sweet of her," she said. "I really do need to go… I have several errands I should get done today."

"Syd, we need to talk…," he said gently tugging on her arm attempting to stop her from running.

"No, we don't...," she said, moving out of his grasp and out the door.

She said a silent prayer of gratitude that she made it to the car without breaking down into a puddle of tears. The show of strength lasted until she was out of sight and then she was forced to pull over and ride out the tide of emotion that swamped her.

*****

"Who gave that woman my address?" Lane demanded, walking into Jett's house later that afternoon.

"I did. She was so sweet and wanted to surprise you with breakfast as a thank you for last night," Clementine said with a huge knowing smile.

"Next time, please ask my permission first. I have no intention of introducing Sophie to every woman I date," Lane said through clenched teeth diligently trying to rein in his temper.

"Speaking of Sophie, did you leave her in the car?"

"No, I put her on the couch as I came through," he said, still irritated. His mood had been soured by the interruption of Meghan and Sydney's abrupt departure that morning. Meghan had brought a variety of bagels and different flavors of cream cheese from a specialty shop near her apartment. In all truth, he hadn't even remembered the conversation about the store, but so much had transpired he did not doubt her version of events. It was a nice thought, but the fact that she would, after a single date, burst in on him without invitation seemed a bit pushy.

Meghan had all but ignored Sophie as they ate their bagels, and Sophie had acted up, apparently picking up on the strange vibes in the house. Between the tantrum throwing toddler and his terse responses to her questions, they had cut breakfast short after less than an hour.

"So, are you really mad at me about the Meghan thing?" Clementine asked coming to stand next to him.

"No, but I had company and…," he stopped mid-sentence realizing his faux pas.

"Whoa! What? Who?" Jett interjected.

He shook his head, "It was… Sydney spent the night last night…"

He looked up to notice that both Jett and Clementine were staring at him as if he had just grown a second head.

"I'm sorry... what?" Jett pushed for an explanation.

"Not like *spent the night*... she slept in my bed..."

"What!?" Clementine interjected with shock radiating out from every pore.

He held out his hand to stop her exclamations, and inhaled deeply for patience.

"*Let me finish.* She and Sophie were asleep in my bed when I got home, at 2 a.m. I might add. They had fallen asleep watching a movie and I didn't want to shove her out of the house in the wee hours."

"Whew, okay that makes more sense. I was going to completely fritz out on you for keeping that secret," Clementine said with a crazy facial expression that would have been amusing under any other circumstance.

"You don't think if Sydney and I were involved you would know by now?" he asked a bit brusquer than intended.

"I guess. I just don't understand the preppy guys she goes for... Fletcher for instance," she wrinkled her nose. "Syd, seems to prefer all flash and brains, with no sizzle," she added as her eyes wandered to Jett.

"Who says we would sizzle?" Lane asked before his brain could stop the slippery slope he was navigating.

"Come on! You, Jett and Ryker are the typical reformed bad boys that most girls love to get our hands on, but Syd, not so much. Her guys were the 'graduating with honors' type. Lawyers, doctors, you know." She patted his arm. "Nothing personal, you are going to make Meghan…"

"About Meghan," he interrupted rudely, as her dismissal of any attraction between Sydney and himself was not sitting well with him.

"What about Meghan?" she asked cautiously.

"That's not going to fly… I appreciate the effort… but…"

"I thought maybe this morning...?" Clementine moved her shoulders and eyes to indicate she thought something of a personal nature might have occurred.

"Nope. We went out *one time*, and she shows up at my door the very next morning?" He hoped his expression filled in the blanks for her, that he was not kosher with that much togetherness that quickly.

"A bit stalker-like, babe… I told you," Jett said winding his arm around Clementine's waist.

"Yeah, I didn't feel it with the two of you last night either. Well, I have one more option…," Clementine immediately switched gears.

"No. I'm good."

After the drama that had unfolded in his kitchen that morning, he didn't want any part of a woman in his life. He didn't understand all the conflicting messages his brain was ticking off on him these days, but he liked his calm existence and didn't need any more chaos.

"Come on man, look at how many frogs I had to kiss before I found my princess," Jett said looking down at Clementine.

Clementine was glaring at him, which choked a laugh out of Lane.

"Just how many princesses *did* you kiss before me?" Clementine crossed her arms and waited.

Lane almost spit his drink out at that one, but remained silent wanting to see how Jett would get out of the predicament.

"Sweetie, you know I was just searching for you… I don't even remember…"

"Liar," she said unwinding her limbs and walking a few steps away.

"Thanks!" Jett shot Lane a death glare.

"What did I do?" He asked trying hard not to let his grin show through.

"Seriously, just one more date and I will let it go if this one doesn't work."

"Okay, one more… and that's it."

"Deal," Clementine fairly skipped away from him.

"Are Darby and Ryker coming down today?"

"Yep, Darby has a dress fitting and we are meeting Sydney downtown to pick up a few things for centerpieces."

"Oh, Syd is not coming here?"

"Nope, she has a big dinner date after we are done."

He schooled his features to not give away anything, but based on the earlier conversation, they wouldn't believe him anyway. The scene in his kitchen had continued to dog every step he took all day. No matter how hard he tried he could not banish it. He would need to talk to Sydney and put things right, but before he could do that, he had to make sense of it all with himself.

CHAPTER 5

Sydney tried to view the arrangement from one side, adjusted the flowers slightly and tried another vantage point. After a long week of back to back clients and meetings, trying to figure out a simple table centerpiece had seemed like a good stress relieving idea. But her perfectionist spirit was not making it any easier than an hour session with a traumatized six year old had been earlier in the day.

"What did that centerpiece ever do to you?" Lane's chuckling question caused her to glance up at him with confusion.

"I just can't get it right, it's too fussy or something," she said frowning as she turned her attention back to the project at hand.

"I think it looks great, but is that bow on the glass thing necessary?"

"You think it's too much?"

He quirked his face in a way that answered her question without words.

Moving forward, she gingerly lifted the large bow off the glass vase and stepped back. He was right! It was perfect!

"I love it. What do you think?"

"It's much cleaner." He said thoughtfully. "I like it. But why are you and not the bride doing this?"

"It's one of the many joys of Maid of Honor duty. As Best Man you don't have any odious tasks you aren't appreciative of being saddled with?"

"Nope, bachelor party and do everything you tell me to… I got it covered," he grinned at her.

She rolled her eyes at him.

"Come on now, I know you enjoy bossing us all around."

"That I do, but carrying the entire weight of Clementine's wedding is not something I want on my conscience if something goes wrong," she huffed out an exasperated breath.

"I have faith in you and I know Clementine does, you don't understand how to fail. Besides, you thrive under pressure."

"Thanks for the vote of confidence. I'm certain you didn't come over just for that though. Did you need something?"

He stepped into the room and out of the doorway.

"Clementine said you volunteered to watch Sophie tonight. Are you sure you don't have plans? I hate to take up two Friday nights in a row."

"No, I'm good," Sydney said, trying to keep her breathing normal. The thought of last Friday night conjured images better left buried deep in her psyche never to be brought up again.

"Okay. I know Sophie loves spending time with you, but I don't want to monopolize your free time. With the wedding and everything I know…"

She cut him off mid-sentence. "If you don't want me to watch her while you go out on your stupid date, I don't have to," Sydney snapped. She wasn't certain where the harsh words came from and she couldn't look at him. Turning toward her desk she attempted to put distance between them.

"Syd?"

She kept walking, turning only when she heard her office door close. Lane was making quick progress across her carpet.

"I'm sorry that... it's been a tough week and I shouldn't have snapped at you."

"Yes, you should have. I don't think this is about your week though. We haven't had a single moment alone at all this week and I think we need to discuss what happened...," he stopped. and she watched his Adam's apple bobble nervously as he swallowed down embarrassment.

"No, we definitely don't need to discuss that... EVER..."

"Sydney, you and I are friends and I don't want anything to come between us. I overstepped last week. I have no excuse."

"I was there too, remember? I don't want this to come between us either, Lane. I promise, it's ok."

"Really? You do understand that you have been staring at that carpet like it has a huge stain on it, and you haven't made direct eye contact since I came in the room."

She lifted her eyes to his. For a moment, they just stared at each other.

"We are good," she said at last, softly.

"Good. I know you are with Fletcher. I'm just going out, having a little fun...," he stated with a small smile.

The mention of Fletcher caused a flash of guilt to ricochet through her. They had ended their relationship when after two heart to heart conversations it was obvious they were not going to be able to make things work. A fact she had not shared with Clementine, much less Lane, and she wasn't about to bring up the subject at that point.

"I understand. We were both tired and it was just a random, thing... but we are good."

"I need you to know, I'm not even certain that I'm ready for some big relationship. And I can't risk us doing something that we both regret down the road and then losing our friendship in the mix."

"Agreed. Besides, I love spending time with Sophie and I wouldn't want that to be jeopardized," she said bolstering his case.

"You are sure?"

"Yes, and I think you are going to really enjoy Rachel. I like her more than Meghan." She tried to sound cheery. "She is down to earth, smart... well, she's a pediatrician so of course she's smart. And stunning... she did a little modeling to pay her way through college. But she also is really nice... she's a good fit for you. And I'm sure Sophie will love her." She realized she was rambling and stopped talking.

"First off, I think we need to wait more than one date this time to introduce her to Sophie. Second, I am only doing this because I promised Clementine to give her one last shot at finding me someone. I liked Meghan, but there just wasn't anything…" he said with an indecisive twist to his mouth.

"You need to wait until someone makes you feel completely happy and alive. You had that with Sarah, and you deserve to find that again," she said sincerely.

"Thanks!"

She took a step back when he took one forward and looked poised to hug her. She might agree to babysit and maintaining a strong friendship, but touching the man again was her kryptonite and not something she could afford to repeat. He must have gotten the message because he stopped mid-stride and backed up two steps.

"Okay then," Lane said, turning to exit. "I will see you around seven?"

"Seven," she said as he slipped from the room.

She sat down hard on her chair. She had dreaded that conversation, but now that it was over all she wanted to do was cry. She knew it was the right decision, the grown-up decision, but she still didn't have to like it. She understood that Lane was just testing the water right now. He was right if he found out it was too soon or he couldn't get over Sarah she did not want their friendship to be a casualty. Her relationship with him, Sophie, Jett, Clementine and even Darby and Ryker were hanging in the balance. One mind-blowing kiss just couldn't outweigh that.

Swiping angrily at the tears, she squared her shoulders and stood. There were a million and one wedding details, a toddler needing her and a business to balance. She couldn't take the time to worry about her sad personal life at this juncture.

*****

Lane focused on the bowling pins at the end of the lane ahead of him. Jett had won the first game and was bragging non-stop. If he wanted to ever hear the end of it, then Lane had to make a good showing this time around. Squaring up, he paced out the steps and with perfect form let the ball fly down the highly shined floor. Watching and willing the ball into position, his arm aimed high when the strike became reality.

"Awesome," Rachel said getting in on the celebration with a fist pump in the air.

Clementine high fived him despite the death glare from Jett. He made sure he swaggered past their chairs just a little more pronounced than was necessary. He knew he would need to repeat the performance several times over to beat Jett, but he would relish the little victories in the meantime. Sitting on a chair two over from Rachel, he swigged his drink and looked toward Clementine now giving her best at adding to her score.

"So, Clementine told me that you run a security business. Like security systems for homes?" Rachel asked looking at him sweetly.

She was a cute blonde, about five foot seven he would guess and was friendly but not aggressive like Meghan. She had dressed for a more casual date in jeans, a loose shirt and flats. When asked about bowling she had immediately seemed into it and was giving as good as she got with the group, like she had been a part of it for a long time. Without trying to quantify the statement, he felt like they could be friends, where that hadn't seemed possible with Meghan.

"Not exactly. Did Clementine tell you that Jett and I served in the military together?"

"Yes, she gave me a brief history," Rachel qualified.

"Well, we now subcontract jobs in that capacity and consult on security clearances, and other client needs."

"Is that what you did in the military?" Rachel asked completely tuned in on him.

"We can't tell you that," Jett said coming over to them, "or we would have to kill you." He grinned. "I think you missed that strike," he said smugly slapping Lane's shoulder.

"Was he serious?" Rachel asked.

"We just can't talk about what we did. We were in a covert branch. I'd better go get his ego back under control," he said stepping forward.

He heard her ask Clementine if they were kidding. Grinning as he heard Clementine confirm their story, he put that out of his mind and focused on the task ahead. One additional strike later and he took up his position next to Rachel.

"You sure you don't want to try again?"

"I'm thinking not, I twisted that ankle good the first game. I'm sorry I'm such a poor help for your team," she said stating the facts without emotion.

"Nothing doing, I can handle Jett."

"So, you have a daughter?" she asked tuning back in to him, obvious interest in her eyes.

"Sophie, will be two in September."

"I was sorry to hear about your wife. I remember when all that was in the news last year. It was heartbreaking," she said with genuine empathy on her face.

"Thanks. It's been tough, but I have great friends that have provided me lots of support and help. I wouldn't have made it with a baby through this without them."

"So is Sophie with a babysitter tonight?"

"No. Sydney stayed with her. She is my go to and has made it possible for me not to have to hire a stranger to care for Sophie when I'm not there."

"Oh..." she suddenly looked off strangely. "Now that all makes sense."

"Did I miss something?"

"I know Sydney, but over the last year she has called me about rashes, sleep patterns and growth of toddler odds and ends. She must spend a lot of time with you and your daughter," she looked at him with an openly curious face.

"Yeah, she and Clementine share an office building with us. She kind of came as a package deal when Jett started dating Clementine. She and my wife... they really hit it off. And since then, she has helped out when I travel, have meetings or just need an extra set of hands. Sometimes my mother comes in for a weekend, too, but usually it is Syd who helps with Sophie."

"So you must know Fletcher?"

He didn't like the way his stomach felt at the mention of the other man.

"We've met."

"Doesn't seem like the two of you would have a lot in common?" She said with blatant curiosity.

"No, but he's been to some cookouts with Sydney. He's a good guy. How do you know him?"

"He... he's our medical supplier at the clinic. He stops in weekly to bring us samples, stock our on-site meds and things like that. I believe it is how he and

Sydney met, when he did the same for the clinic she interned at before starting her practice."

"Small world," he said examining his drink.

"You're up," Jett said, looking dejected. Lane glanced up and saw three pins standing and jumped up gleefully at the chance to increase his lead.

He was having a nice enough time and decided that he could see himself asking Rachel out for another date. That was progress he thought, now he just needed to make sure he got out of the game with his pride intact. Bragging rights over Jett was just going to be icing on the cake!

CHAPTER 6

Three weeks later, Sydney was balancing on one of the folding chairs trying to figure out how to attach the little streamers from the ceiling tiles. She could barely reach and decided she would need to find a taller chair or maybe a ladder if she wasn't going to injure herself decorating. She jumped down and ran to the utility closet off the kitchen of the rented space. Opening the door she hit pay dirt when her eyes alighted on the step ladder leaning against one of the walls. Grabbing it up she took off at a clip to the main room. She had a million things to do and definitely not enough time to manage it all. She sincerely hoped some of Clementine's other friends who said they might show up would make good on their promises.

"Whoa, slow down there speedy," Lane said, stopping her short.

"Lane," she said dazed. "What are you doing here?"

"I asked him to tag along so that we could get everything done more quickly. Thought I might steal him for lunch afterward," Rachel said, holding Lane's arm and leaning up for a kiss.

As he bent his head, Sydney turned sharply from the scene. She had heard that he and Rachel had been out a number of times. Hearing rumors and having to watch them make-out in front of her were two very different things.

"Sorry, I just can't keep my hands off his fine body," Rachel said with a gush. "What can I help with?"

"Streamers. I need to get these all…"

"I got that," Lane volunteered before she had to detail what was needed further.

"Oh, honey, that is a woman's thing," Rachel said in a girly voice.

"Sydney has me well trained," he said gruffly. "Tell her. Syd."

"I have put his height to good use once or twice," she acknowledged.

"Then what can I do to help?" Rachel asked.

"I have table clothes, place settings and decorations over there," Sydney pointed to the boxes lined up just inside the front door.

"Okay. I will start setting up the tables."

"Great, and I will get the little goodie bags organized. I finished shopping for everything last night but didn't have time to assemble them," she said, stopping as several other women entered.

She watched Rachel who seemed acquainted with everyone give directions. It was obvious that Rachel was a bigger extrovert than Sydney and adept at fitting into any social situation in which she found herself. As the group giggled and went about their various assignments, Sydney headed to the workroom just off of the main room where she had started laying out the items for the gift bags.

One by one soaps, lotions and other small trinkets were laid out. She had confirmed attendees of thirty and so had planned to make forty bags just to be on the safe side. Setting to work, she didn't hear a noise until Lane was directly next to her.

"What's wrong?" Lane asked in a hushed tone.

"Nothing. Just a lot to get done," she said keeping her hands busy and not looking up.

"Syd, don't try to start lying to me now," he said patiently.

She looked up at him.

"I'm really okay, just…" she looked out at the other room. "They all are so bubbly and happy. Clementine is getting married and is the same way these days. I just feel a bit… overwhelmed."

"You take on a lot. You are the organizer in our group, and everyone just lets you do everything because it's what you are good at but sometimes they forget to show their gratitude."

"It's not that," she sighed. "It's nothing."

"Is it Rachel?"

"No, you guys seem happy together. Clementine told me things are going great on that front. I'm so happy you found someone that you are getting on with…," she sighed and tried to keep the tears threatening at bay.

"It's been three weeks, don't go planning my wedding yet," he said gruffly.

"But you are happy and having fun… right?"

He just stared at her a minute before carefully answering.

"She's funny, smart and fun to be with."

She squinted at him, "But?"

"No but, I just…"

"Lane, what'cha doing in here?" Rachel asked moving into the room to stand alongside of him.

"Talking with Sydney."

"I think we can have this done pretty quickly with all the hands helping. Hurry up and finish the streamers so we can go," she said, batting her eyelashes up at him.

"Yes, ma'am!" he turned just slightly back to Sydney. "I've been given my marching orders."

"That you have," she said, watching him and his girlfriend walk out of the room.

She turned back to her project. She had a party to plan and busy hands ensured she didn't try and dissect Lane or think about him at all. *Yeah, right*!

*****

Lane watched Rachel trying to draw Sophie's attention to something the mother orangutan was doing. She was minimally successful as the toddler, and she took off for another window to see the monkey that was right against the pane. He realized it was probably too soon for him to be introducing Sophie to another woman, but he was away from her all week and didn't want to miss the weekend, too. Besides, the zoo was as innocuous of a place as any to just have a "friend" tag along and test the waters with Sophie.

"She is definitely busy," Rachel said, grinning at the little girl as she came to stand next to him.

"That little brain never takes a break, unless she is sleeping," he agreed.

"Daa..." Sophie turned to him and made a motion that she wanted him to come.

Rachel walked beside him over to where Sophie stood. She was aggressively poking the glass trying to get him to see something.

"I see, honey," he said bending down to her. A moment later she appeared to forget he was there, and he stood to give Rachel some attention.

"So I was thinking..." she said running her hand up his arm.

He stared at the arm. It felt nice to have someone holding on to him, and he was definitely warming up to Rachel. Still no fireworks, but there was a growing attraction developing and he was enjoying the new sensations. To date, he hadn't found anything that they disagreed upon, and she was allowing him to drive the pace he was comfortable with.

"Am I going to like this thinking?" he asked with a squint.

"I hope so. Do you think you could get a babysitter for an entire weekend for Sophie?"

"I could, but I won't."

"I'm sorry?"

"I am away from her all week, as it is. I can't be away all weekend, too," he responded decidedly.

"Okay, what about one night?"

"Maybe, what did you have in mind?"

"I have tickets for Miranda Lambert in Houston and thought we might make a weekend of it?"

"When is it?"

"Next weekend?"

"That's a week before Clementine's wedding."

"I know, and I checked with her. She said the rehearsal dinner is the Friday after and there is stuff to do that week but thought it was a great idea for the weekend."

"We have only been dating three weeks?"

"Four when we are there... how long do you normally wait?"

"I'm sorry... are we having this conversation right now?" he asked glancing over at Sophie.

"I just want you to know you have a green light, and I'm game," she said tipping her face up as if she wanted a kiss.

He gave her a peck, and pulled back.

"Just think about it," she said and then moved forward to rejoin Sophie.

Three weeks was long enough? He definitely was getting old and was a bit more old-fashioned than he had originally thought. He wanted to know for sure a relationship was going some place before jumping into bed with a woman. And why go out of town? What if it was a bust? What if Sophie needed him? He most

Angelica Kate -- 97

certainly couldn't ask Sydney… she would know why and that was just… WRONG.

Deciding he needed to breathe, he gathered Sophie up with the promise of elephants. Rachel must have sensed his mood, because she didn't talk as she walked next to the stroller.

"Fletcher!" Rachel suddenly called out of the blue.

Turning, he caught sight of the man in question coming forward, with a woman that was most assuredly not Sydney.

"Annabeth," he watched Rachel fling her arms around the other woman.

"Lane," Fletcher came up to him and extended his hand.

"Fletcher, what is going on?" he asked in a low threatening tone, looking from him to the woman.

Fletcher looked him square in the eye.

"Didn't Sydney tell you? We broke up almost a month ago now."

Lane felt the pit of his stomach drop to the path on which he stood. That would mean close to or the exact day of the kitchen episode. *Oh no, it was his fault*!

"I'm sorry…why?"

"We just found that we weren't compatible in certain critical areas. I am surprised she didn't tell you, considering..." he shook his head and didn't finish the thought.

It *was* because of him, Lane thought.

"Lane, this is Annabeth. She and Fletcher dated back in college, and I guess when Sydney and him broke up they reconnected."

"It's nice meeting you," Annabeth said.

"And you," he reciprocated.

The rest of the conversation faded into buzzing noises as his brain tried to process the information overload. Even Sophie was getting fussy, and them having to move on to the next exhibit couldn't completely break him loose of the fog. He needed to talk to Sydney. He had to make this right!

*****

Sydney padded across the living room balancing the remote and bowl of ice cream in one hand and her warm fuzzy blanket in the other with a DVD copy of *The Proposal*. She was prepared for a chick flick and a snooze after a long weekend. She had run eight miles, done laundry, cut her lawn and thrown a bridal shower. In her opinion, she had earned the treat and movie.

Putting the bowl on the coffee table, she walked over and flicked on the television, powered up the DVD player and waited for the tray to accept the movie. As the green preview screen lit up her living room, she plodded back to the sofa. Rolling her shoulders, she sat down and picked up the bowl of ice cream.

DING DONG

She glanced over to the front entrance and tried to surmise who would be on the other side of the door. She knew Clementine was planning to clean tonight and hadn't indicated stopping over when she talked to her an hour or so ago. Her brain didn't come up with any other possibilities. Assuming it was probably a sales person, she decided to ignore the intrusion.

DING DONG

Picking up the remote she hit the "pause" button, and with a small sigh she stood up.

"This better be life and death," she mumbled to herself.

Unlocking the deadbolt, she opened the door. Whatever her brain had been about to formulate in response to the visitor fled.

"Lane! What are you doing here?" she asked with concern.

Lane never came over unannounced, and especially in the evening because it was so close to Sophie's bedtime.

"We need to talk," he said and pushed past her.

"Come in," she said, confused, stepping out of his way. She glanced toward the truck parked in her drive to see if Rachel was with him. It was dark and appeared to be empty.

She closed the door and turned. He stood with his head down and was fiddling with his hands.

"Where's Sophie?" she asked breaking the silence.

"Jett is watching her."

She chuckled, "You are feeling brave today aren't you?"

He looked up and smiled, "He needs to learn."

"Probably, considering Clementine wants a big family. So what gives?"

"I… we were at the zoo today, walking the gardens and looking at the animals," he paused.

"Okay, by you I'm assuming you mean Rachel, Sophie and yourself?" she asked.

"Yes, but that isn't the… we ran into Fletcher," he said, capturing her eyes and not wavering.

Crap! It wasn't like she was hiding the fact that she and Fletcher had broken up, it just hadn't seemed relevant. Besides, she felt bad that she was so comfortable with the decision. She had begun to worry there really was something wrong with her, and she wasn't ready for any of her friends to weigh in on the subject. Unfortunately, it would appear *that* reprieve was over.

"What did he tell you?"

"You mean after I got over the shock of him approaching us with another woman? Did you know he was back together with his college girlfriend Annabeth?"

"Yes, I'd heard," she said smoothly.

"He said you broke up a month ago."

"Yes."

"It wasn't around the time of… you know… our thing… that morning with Meghan," he was getting flushed and obviously struggling to coherently communicate.

"It was not because of our stupid kiss, Lane. It was the same day, but it was an appointment of sorts we had already set before any of that happened."

"Our *stupid kiss*," he said wiping a hand over his face turning away from her.

"We agreed to not discuss it again. It happened and we can't let it get in the way of us being friends, remember? *You* are the one that gave me that speech?"

"I remember," he turned around to her. "Why did you break up then?"

She sighed, wishing for the first time in her life she was a better liar. Something about her face when she did try to tell even a little a white lie by omission always gave her away.

"He had asked that I not spend as much time with… Sophie. He thought I was getting too attached."

"Sophie?"

"Yes."

She didn't add that Lane had been included in the request. Fletcher had felt that with her constant attentiveness to Lane and his daughter she was short changing the time he should be given. He wanted to lap up all her attention and put the work in to make their relationship grow. Something in his tone hadn't set well with Sydney, and she couldn't meet his demands. In the end, she pulled the plug on their relationship. Knowing that he had gone back to Annabeth inside of ten days said that it had been the right choice.

"I was worried that it had something to do with me. I would never want to do anything that might hinder your happiness."

"After all the time we spent together, something was still missing. It worked out the way it was meant to," she said, trying to give Lane the reassurance he needed.

She looked at him, and he crooked his neck slightly as if trying to figure something out from her facial features.

"Did you guys ever do a weekend away, together? I can't remember that happening, but then I don't know every move you make?"

She laughed nervously, trying to catch up to the sudden change of subject.

"No, we didn't. Why?"

"Rachel, wants me to go to Houston with her for a concert and overnight getaway next weekend," he said, suddenly sitting down on the chair next to her couch.

"Wow! You guys are moving fast!"

"Thank you," he said looking relieved. "That's how I feel, but seriously, I have never had a relationship besides Sarah. We met in high school, so things were different those days."

"You are a big grown up now." She grinned at him going around the coffee table to sit on the corner of the sofa. She laid a hand on his leg, "Lane, only you know what you are and aren't comfortable with. You are putting yourself out there, but that doesn't mean anyone can dictate how fast or on what timeline your relationship should move forward."

He put his hand down on top of hers and sat silently for a moment.

"I do like Rachel. She's not as aggressive as Meghan or others I have met. She's smart, easy to talk to, and she got along great with Sophie at the zoo yesterday. But it's been… it's just not long enough for me to know if I want to take that next step."

"Tell her that. I know Rachel and I truly believe she will understand. Besides, we have a ton of stuff with the wedding coming in the next two weeks… you can put her off with that for a little while."

He looked up at her, and she had the sudden urge to put her hand on his cheek. That picture was quickly replaced with other images of things she would like to do with him. Pulling her hand back, she realized that whatever her strange new attraction to Lane was she needed to keep her distance until it was extinguished. He had Rachel now, and they were friends. He was her family, and she wouldn't allow anything to interfere with that relationship, even her own crazy feelings.

"Thank you, Syd," he said rising from the chair.

"Anytime," she said standing to follow him.

When they got to the door, he opened it wide. She moved forward to close it behind him, and then, without warning, he turned and pulled her into a big hug. She closed her eyes as her head rested on his chest and clung to him for a moment, savoring the embrace while it lasted.

"Night, Syd," he said, breaking the contact and quickly walking out the door.

"Night," she whispered into the night. She stood staring into the darkness, long after he drove away.

There went her restful night! Her body was firing on all pistons. She headed to her bathroom, and opted for a cold shower instead of the ice cream and a movie. *Damn the man!*

CHAPTER 7

Lane stared at the door Rachel had just left through. She had stopped by to get his answer about the coming weekend, and while disappointed, she had appeared understanding about his declining the invitation. Another friend of hers was going to take his ticket, and she recovered quickly from his refusal. He waited to see if regret crowded his mind, but all he felt was relief.

Within a week, family and friends would start arriving, rehearsal dinner next Friday and then a weekend of celebration. He and Sophie were both in the wedding party, so they were included in all activities. Besides,

Sydney had so many details to attend to, he had to ensure that he kept lending a hand wherever needed.

The other big event was the bachelor party, slated for Friday evening. He knew the owner of a bar downtown who had agreed to close for the private party. Nothing wild or crazy. No strippers, he had decided, although knowing some of the guys flying in he wouldn't put it past them to do something completely off the charts. It was one more reason why he hadn't felt comfortable going away for the weekend.

Not certain if Rachel would reach out and talk to Clementine or Sydney, he decided to talk to them when he got to the office.

Clementine's office door was closed and the "In Session" light was on, but he did hear faint noises coming from Sydney's office. He walked in that direction, stopping short when he heard Rachel's voice.

"I'm just afraid he isn't capable of loving someone again this soon," Rachel complained.

"Sweetie, Lane has a huge heart. I can assure you he is capable of loving someone again. Our hearts expand to include friends, lovers and family in whatever quantity we are given. I have faith that Lane will find someone to share the rest of his life with and love deeply."

"More than Sarah?" Rachel asked.

Lane knew he should move, but couldn't.

"No, not *more* than Sarah. She was his first crush, his high school sweetheart, the reason he could run into terrible combat situations with humanity, and the mother of his daughter. She will always hold those places in his heart. The love he will feel for someone else will be different, but it will be complete and faithful. He will love her for all the joy she brings to his and Sophie's world. She will be blessed by helping him raise Sophie, giving him additional children, being his helpmate, and lover. All the memories that will be uniquely theirs. That is a love that will be as strong as the one he had with Sarah, just different."

"I don't know if I can play second fiddle," Rachel said.

"I think if you believe you are second fiddle, then there is a problem. Neither of you should feel you are settling. You need to know in your heart that this is the person you were meant to be with."

Lane was humbled by Sydney's words. *She just got it.* She was able to put into words what he wanted and wasn't able to craft verbally for Rachel. He wasn't looking for someone to replace Sarah but for someone who would share the rest of his life and love him and allow him to reciprocate, but she would definitely need to understand the unique spot Sarah would always occupy in his heart. Sydney got that, and he was grateful for her trying to make Rachel comprehend such a heartrending subject.

"Would it be enough for you?" Rachel asked unexpectedly.

Lane felt the breathe whoosh out of his lungs and he suspended there waiting. He needed to move. He shouldn't want to overhear her response. His feet were concrete blocks though, and his brain couldn't make them move.

"Absolutely!" Sydney responded without a moment's hesitation. "Think about it, you get Lane and Sophie in the mix. They are so worth it! Anyone Lane loves will be doted on and taken care of like he does that little girl. It's all I have ever imagined from a great relationship," Sydney said and he could almost imagine the sappy look on her face.

He felt his heart tighten painfully, and then he inhaled, pushed away from the wall and walked back to his office in a daze.

Once inside his office he reached out to the only person he thought could understand the turmoil he was experiencing.

"Sarah, maybe I am rushing this. You heard Rachel, and I must still be giving off vibes of loving you so much that I can't open up. I want to, sweetheart, and I know Sophie could benefit from having a woman around. My brain says I'm ready, but my heart… it's conflicted. I just wish… I wish there was a way you could just give me a sign. Tell me if I'm doing the right thing. What am I missing?"

He sighed. Doubting he would suddenly get the signal he was looking for, he decided that he needed to get a workout in. Grabbing his bag, he headed out to the gym. He could at the very least sweat away a few concerns. Maybe tiring his brain out would be a good thing.

*****

"Oh my goodness, look who's here," Rachel cooed.

"Who?" Sydney asked turning to see where she was looking.

Following her line of sight, she sucked in a breath. There in all their sweaty hot glory were two of the finest specimens of manhood she had seen. The desire to run from the room became so strong she had to strain against the impulse.

"God, he is one fine looking man," Rachel gushed moving a few steps toward Lane and Jett on the weight machine.

"Fancy meeting you here," Jett said looking at her.

"I dragged Sydney along because Clementine had appointments all afternoon. I needed to burn off a little frustration," she said, pointedly looking at Lane.

Sydney almost choked at her forthrightness.

"Rachel…" Lane started at the bold comment.

"I'm just kidding, Lane. Easy boy, I am good with the decision. Sydney and I had a nice long talk." She sidled up to him and ran a hand over his tattooed forearm. "I am willing to wait. I've been assured you are worth it."

Sydney watched Lane's eyes drift over to her, and she tried to plaster an encouraging smile on her face. He looked at her workout clothes as she fought the urge to yank the brief tank top over her spandex workout pants. She despised the reactions rising up in her from a single glance from him.

"Syd," Troy, her trainer, came up behind her. "You want me to spot you through circuit today?"

"That would be great." She turned, grateful for the excuse to leave the uncomfortable gathering. She wouldn't have to watch Rachel continue to flirt openly with Lane. *Lane, her boyfriend*, Sydney reminded herself, to get her brain to forcibly change channels.

Troy walked off toward the first station they normally worked at and she turned to bid a farewell to the group.

"He's super cute," Rachel whispered in her ear.

"He's my *trainer*," she said. Turning to follow Troy she realized that he was aesthetically pleasing, and she could see why some women might find him appealing. It was the first time in over a year of working with him at the gym that she had even noticed. *There really was something wrong with her!*

She began the workout. Within ten minutes she couldn't think about anything but about when the torture would be over. Every few minutes she would glance over to find Rachel, Jett and Lane working out together. She envied Rachel's ability to assimilate so easily into the group, and she was looking trim and pretty in her workout gear, not like her sweaty self.

"Okay, cool down and you are ready to go," Troy said after what she thought was a short time but in reality was forty-five minutes.

After a quick shower and change, she was standing outside of the locker room waiting for Rachel to finish dressing. The men's locker room door opened.

"Hey," Lane said.

"Good workout?" she asked.

"Yeah, Rachel is a talker... didn't get as much done as normal," he said with a slight grin.

"I think you're good," she said looking at his arms.

"Didn't think you noticed," he teased.

"Hard not too when your girlfriend is salivating all over you and rubbing up on those guns without a care to who is around," she said with a sarcastic curl to her mouth.

"She was coming on a bit strong," he said with a chuckle.

"Guys like that, right?"

"Why? You thinking of trying it out?"

"Maybe. As you know, I'm in the market for a new man," she said with what she hoped was a more confident smile than how she was feeling at that moment.

"I guess we like to know where you stand, but sometimes pushy… is just pushy… it's a fine line."

"Good to know."

"You going to make a play for that trainer?" he asked not meeting her eyes.

"No! He's quite a bit younger and can only talk about working out and disc golf," she laughed.

"I bet you could get him to be open to other areas of interest," Lane said encouragingly.

"In case you haven't noticed, I'm not the type of woman that can talk men into things. Maybe if I looked like Rachel…"

"Stop it!" he growled at her. "You may not be flashy beautiful like Clementine or Rachel, but you are perfect just the way you are. If guys can't see that… screw them. The right one will see how beautiful you really are," he bit out. It was the longest speech on the subject he had ever made, and she couldn't help the tiny bubble of happiness it produced.

"Thanks," she said.

"Ready?" Rachel asked, interrupting as she came out of the locker room.

"Yep, see ya, Lanc," Sydney said starting to walk off.

"I will see *you* later," she heard Rachel said in a suggestive tenor.

Sydney refused to turn around and witness a good-bye kiss. She needed to just kept putting one foot in front of the other until she hit the bright sunlight. Only then was she able to inhale her first tension free breathe since they had entered the gym an hour before.

CHAPTER 8

Lane was attempting to keep a clear head as he looked over the gathered group. The innocuous party had gotten out of hand somewhere around hour two. For the most part it was just a bunch of harmless fun, boys being boys trying hard to prove who was superior. Unfortunately, when the darts had come out, the players were a few too many drinks in and someone had gotten hit in the side of the face. He had patched the guy up and was just now returning from putting the first aid kit back when he heard a loud roar and what sounded like women from the main area of the bar.

Please don't let them be strippers. He said a silent prayer and rolling his shoulders back stepped into the crowded room.

Before he made it all the way out, he was accosted by Rachel, pushing him backward, and kissing him without a sound. It took his brain a moment to register that she was at Jett's bachelor party and not Clementine's bachelorette party across town.

"Rachel?" he said pushing her away from him. "Why are you here?"

"Aren't you happy to see me?" she asked, reaching for him again. He licked his lips and tasted the sweet alcohol. That would explain a bit of her aggression, but surely she hadn't driven over by herself.

"I am happy to see you but...," he hesitated looking around at the others that had followed Rachel inside.

"I thought if we couldn't get away for the weekend," she said getting more aggressive in her attempt to draw him to her.

He felt his psyche take a hit, as he realized that he wanted to feel more, but instead of desire, he was feeling somewhat angry. Unfortunately, it was not the time to dissect that as his leadership skills roared fully to life.

"I am glad to see you, but how did you get here?"

"We all decided to crash the party. Sydney's get together was a bit... blah..." she made an odious face.

Oh god, so that was it. Poor Sydney! Clementine had asked for a low key event, but alcohol and peer pressure must have played a part in derailing that.

"We need to go out there and make sure everything is running smoothly," he said drawing her with him.

"And then can we get a little... busy," she whispered.

"We will see," was all he was willing to accede to at the moment.

As they entered the main part of the bar, he was met with double the occupants as had been there a mere ten minutes earlier, and he realized that it had become a co-ed party. He saw Jett and Clementine out on the dance floor slow dancing along with about six other couples. Several women he didn't recognize were ordering drinks at the bar. Everyone seemed to be getting along, and no one seemed put out about the party crashers.

"Can I have this dance," Greg a friend who had served with them directed the question to Rachel.

"Go have some fun," he said when she raised quizzical eyes to him.

"Okee... dokee..." she said and slapped her hand into Greg's outstretched one.

Darby broke loose and headed in his direction. "Sorry to crash the party, but some of these girls are..."

"Crazy," he filled in.

"Exactly, but it all seems like good fun. How are you?" she asked reaching out to hug him.

"Considering that I'm the designated host and driver tonight I feel like a referee of sorts."

"You and Sydney both. No wonder they made the pair of you Maid of Honor and Best Man," she grinned up at him. "Sorry Ryker couldn't join me, but he is working on the new construction project for the farm and they are pouring concrete this weekend."

"Totally understand. He'd better make the wedding though," he said gazing around. He still couldn't lay eyes on Sydney, and that was making him edgy for some reason.

"We both wouldn't miss it for the world. Besides, Clementine has Tyler as one of the ushers. He is so excited about getting to wear his new suit," Darby gushed with beaming motherly pride.

"I'm sure he will look dapper."

Tyler was a foster child Darby had decided to adopt before marrying Ryker. The little boy had been through so much sadness in his short life by the time he had been enrolled in her therapy program. When she had found out that he would be moved to yet another foster home, she had taken him in. She and Ryker were now in the final stages of adopting him, and Clementine had lovingly provided him an "important" job for her wedding.

"Thanks." Darby smiled softly at him. "She's outside," she said thumbing a finger toward the door.

"Sorry?" he asked looking down at her, confused.

"Sydney. You've been looking around for her the entire time we have been talking," she told him with a knowing grin.

"How did you…" he shook his head when Darby just quirked her eyebrow at him.

"Thanks," he said, squeezing her arm as he headed for the door.

He found Sydney sitting inside the back of a limousine parked just outside the bar. Her legs were dangling out the open door, and the sad look on her face tugged at him. He crossed to the car.

"Move over," he said ducking down.

She looked up at him with tear-brightened eyes but silently slid over on the seat. He climbed inside and closed the door.

Without a word, she buried her face in his shirt and he wrapped his arms around her as she cried out all her frustration. *For someone who put on such a tough persona for the world, the woman was a big marshmallow inside.*

*****

Sydney hadn't meant to let anyone know how upset the unwinding of the evening's events had made her. She had been getting some fresh air and bolstering her spirits to join the group inside when Lane appeared. The man seemed to have an uncanny way of figuring her out and showing up when she was the most vulnerable.

She gulped in air, and tried for the third time to stop the deluge of tears. Leaning back from Lane's warm chest, she looked up at him and then back at the massive wet spot on the front of his dress shirt.

"I'm so sorry, I don't know where that all came from," she said, wiping her eyes with the hanky he had produced.

"What happened tonight?" he questioned, gently pushing a stray hair back from her face.

"I don't know. We had dinner and were all settling in talking, when several of the women asked about strippers. Seriously, strippers?" she rolled her eyes at him. "You were there. Clementine said a quiet dinner with all her girlfriends."

"Yes, she did. But, sweetie," he reached up and wiped a tear off her cheek. "You went to school with some of those women. You have told me horror stories about their wild parties back in the day. Leopards don't just change their spots with age."

"I was not part of that group back then. I always heard about them second hand. I have to admit, I thought most of it was just boasting," she said with a huff. "Then this limo showed up and they democratically decided to go for a ride. Somewhere along the drive... Jett's party came up... and here we are," she shrugged.

"You know you aren't ever getting them out of there now," he said with an upturn of one side of his mouth.

She hated that that the party she had planned for weeks was so boring that no one had wanted to stay. She wished she had thought to add enough activities to keep all of Clementine's guests happy, but she had foolishly thought that just having time to catch up with Clementine would be enough. She had obviously underestimated the lot of her friends.

"Did Rachel find you?" Rachel had barreled out of the limo like she was on fire, in search of Lane she had said. From the look in her eyes and the fact that she had already had too much to drink, the message was loud and clear.

"Oh yeah," he said averting his eyes.

The action caused her to laugh.

"She attacked did she?"

"That is definitely one way of describing it. I didn't see this side of her personality, but she has decided... well..." he cleared his throat.

She caught herself laughing aloud at his discomfort. "She thinks you're sexy... she wants your body..." she sang at him.

"I think you stole that from a movie," he said blandly.

"Come on, you have to be flattered by the attention."

"I am, but I... remember telling me that you thought you were broken?" he asked looking out the window.

"Yeah."

"I just don't... I can't get myself to that point with her. This is what I was worried about, that I just couldn't..." he made a motion above his heart.

"She's not asking for your heart right now... just some fun... the rest will work itself out,' she looked at him seriously. "And there is nothing that says if it makes you uncomfortable, you can't just stop and wait a while."

"Maybe," he said. "You okay now about this?" he pointed to the party raging inside the establishment they were outside of at the moment.

"I just don't want Clementine to think I let her down."

"She knows how much you have done for her wedding. I don't think that thought will cross her mind in the least."

"Thank you," she said leaning forward to hug him. She didn't filter this one but instead wrapped herself into the warmth of his understanding.

As quick as it began, she backed up and pulled the door release. A moment later, they were outside the car.

"Now, let's go have some fun," he said.

Once inside, the party atmosphere seeped into her bones, and soon she couldn't help but loosen up. Two tequila shots and one tube of a blue concoction later she was dancing with a complete stranger and enjoying it! As the music slowed, Rachel sidled up alongside her with Lane in tow.

"You having fun?" Rachel slurred a bit with a cheesy grin.

"Yep," Sydney said, swaying, anchored to the big sailor fellow named Terry.

"Switch partners," Terry said suddenly letting her go as Rachel gamely took her place.

"I guess it's you and me," said Lane as she stepped into his arms.

"You not worried about Rashel..." she asked looking up at him with a big grin.

"Syd, honey, how many drinks did you have?"

"Two..," she showed him by holding up two fingers. "Oh, plus one little tube," she squinted her eyes trying to measure with her forefinger and thumb exact size of the tube.

"Do you want to sit down?" Lane said with a little chuckle.

"No!" She said wiggling into him closer, resting her head on his wide chest and snuggling in. "I want your warmth," she said into his shirt.

"Umm… hmmm," he answered bringing his arms around her tighter.

She felt like her brain was turned off and the filter on her thoughts and emotions gone. The euphoric state was a nice place to visit she thought, soaking up Lane's heat.

She slipped her hand braced against his chest up higher on his person and found her finger accidentally between the buttons under her cheek. She moved her fingers over the warm hot flesh, and prickly hairs she found, but she didn't immediately remove her hand to safe territory. The hiss he let loose had her pulling her heavy head back and looking up at him. She remembered that stormy look in his eyes. Testing the water she moved her fingers on the inside of his shirt, her motion fueled by the sense of power over the big man her two little fingers seemed to have. She felt the shock to her toes and couldn't in her current state rationally talk herself out of the action. His breathing changed to match her short heaving breaths.

He pulled her against him and bent down, "Syd, you need to stop that now or we are going to cause a scene on this dance floor," he hissed into her ear.

"Didja know, Rashel isn't the only one that thinks you're sexy," she sighed standing on her toes to whisper in his ear.

He grabbed both her hands at that point and dragged her off the dance floor into a corner of the bar.

"Sydney, you need to leave the alcohol alone," he started, but didn't get further as Rachel came up and looped an arm through his.

"Come finish the dance with me," she said her bottom lip protruding just enough to be cute.

Sydney watched Lane allow himself to be lead off the dance floor. She watched them go, trying to read what he was thinking as he turned one final time to check on her. Her sloshy brain wasn't processing at the moment, turning to the bar tender she inquired after some coffee to help reactivate her rational side.

CHAPTER 9

The rehearsal dinner venue was a local steakhouse, and the banquet room they had reserved was already brimming with people when Lane walked in with Sophie and Rachel. Looking around, he caught Jett's eyes and a motion of the hand instructing him to the other end of the table. He put his arm around Rachel to shepherd her the correct path.

Sophie fussed in his arms.

"What's wrong sweet girl?" he asked noticing her binky was not in its usual spot in her mouth.

"I have her," Rachel said reaching up to take the toddler.

"She needs her binky. I must have left it at home." He stated absently patting his pockets were he normally stashed one when they were going out in public.

"I think it was on the kitchen counter. I didn't think to grab it," Rachel responded worriedly. She was rocking Sophie back and forth on her hip, but the toddler was not settling.

"It's okay." He looked around. "If I can find some crackers, then I can stave off her crankiness. It is almost her bedtime, and tomorrow is a big day so I'm hoping she will settle and maybe sleep."

"Good luck, it's pretty noisy in here."

"I have to go see what Jett needs. Are you sure you are okay with her?" Lane turned worriedly in Rachel's direction.

"I am a pediatrician, Lane. I deal with cranky kids all day long. Go," she said playfully pushing him.

As he walked forward, he noticed Sydney to one side deep in conversation with Clementine's mom. They hadn't talked since Friday night, except for a few brief words about the wedding. She looked beautiful in a flowing pink concoction, one beaded bracelet and flats. It appeared she had applied make-up and was looking every part the gracious host for the evening. Such a dinner party was so much more her style of event than the co-ed party that had continued into the wee hours Saturday. The thought of that party brought back to mind the episode on the dance floor. He had worked to erase the memory, to no avail. His sincere hope was Sydney didn't recall the specifics. He just needed things to get back to normal with her, and the uneasy feelings churning inside to subside.

Jett slugged him in the arm bringing him up short at just that moment.

"Hey, you should have brought Rachel and Sophie. We saved seats for everyone in the wedding tomorrow on this end of the room."

"Okay, we will make our way over. Sophie's binky got left at home, and we are trying to get her settled."

"No worries, a screaming kid will just add to the stories," Jett said good-naturedly.

"Thanks. Anything else I can do?"

"No. Sydney, as usual, has everything including my lovely bride well in hand," Jett said nodding to toward the woman of hour.

Lane turned around, and caught Sydney talking to Rachel and Sophie. As he made his way across the room again, stopping for the occasional introduction and brief conversation he kept his ears peeled for Sophie's screams should Rachel need rescuing.

"Hey," he came up next to Rachel finally. "We have a spot at the front."

"Okay," she said giving him an indescribable glance.

"What?"

She nodded down at Sophie who was laying her head on Rachel's shoulder.

"Aww, that's great. Thanks…"

"Not that," she turned slightly and there in Sophie's peaceful face was showcased a binky.

"Where did you find it?"

"I didn't. *Sydney* had one in her purse," she said with a strange look on her face,

"Okay, what's the problem then?"

"Why does Sydney keep supplies for Sophie in her purse?"

"Because she has her a lot, I guess," he said off handed, not certain why Rachel had the bewildered look on her face.

"I know that, but… never mind."

"You know Sydney, she's the typical girl scout with a side of OCD. Be grateful she had one, it will make tonight MUCH easier."

"Right. Johnny on the spot! Always there to take care of Sophie… and you!"

He didn't want to have that conversation with her. It was not the time or the place.

"She has helped *a lot* this past year, and I'm not going to question something as mundane as a binky," he whispered trying to stave off what appeared on the verge of a full blown adult tantrum. He was confused and needing her to calm down here in public.

"Fine," she said moving in front of him. She walked briskly toward the front of the room where Jett had directed them to find a seat. Something in her voice told him she had much more to say one the subject.

Ten minutes later everyone was seated and working through orders. Sophie was on his lap, Rachel's hand on his knee and everything for the moment seemed peaceful and good. Tomorrow would be a great new beginning for one of his brothers, as he thought of Ryker, Jett and even Bryce still. Sarah would have loved this and been right in the thick of things with Sydney planning it all. That thought had him turning to look across the table at the Maid of Honor, deep in conversation with the pastor who would preside over things tomorrow. She was fairly glowing herself with happiness for the happy couple.

"Da… da… da..." Sophie complained.

"Shh… it's okay, baby," he said rubbing her back.

She wiggled around as if trying to find a comfortable spot.

"Do you want to sit in your chair?' he asked indicating the empty one next to him, with a booster seat perched on it.

"No..." she said with a small whimper.

"You want to come to me?" Rachel asked extending her hands.

"No!" she said and pushed the hands away.

"Awww…come on, honey," Rachel tried again.

"No!" Sophie said firmly.

"Sophie," he whispered kissing her head and rocking slightly to calm her. He caught Sydney looking at him anxiously.

"I can take her," Rachel said. "Let me walk her outside for a bit and see if I can settle her," she made to stand up.

"No!" Sophie said. "Nee... neee…"

Rachel yanked her hand back and glanced over at Sydney. Lane followed her gaze and saw the empathy in Sydney's eyes.

"Sophie," he said clearing his throat and trying to soothe her.

The toddler wiggled trying to get down. Not able to control her growing erratic movements, he let her get down and pushed back to follow her out of the room. Running around the table, she suddenly stopped next to Sydney and lifted her arms to be picked up. He watched Sydney raise the body up, and snuggle her whispering tiny words as she rocked his daughter. When turning back to his seat he caught the hurt in Rachel's eyes. He was tired of the drama. He refused to limit someone as important as Sydney to Sophie just to appease a new girlfriend. He would not cause discord at Jett and Clementine's celebration, but after that he was going to need to address it head on.

*****

"You want some help," Darby came up behind Sydney.

"Wow, didn't hear you coming," she turned with a smile.

It was pitch black outside, but she had come over to the wedding venue straight from the rehearsal dinner. She knew she wouldn't be able to sleep, and she had a million little details to have just right by tomorrow at 2 p.m. So, at 9:30 p.m., she was alone decorating tables and trying to wrap her mind around the big event that would take place the next day.

"I knew that I would find you here," Darby said. "You are like me with the details and compulsion to make sure everything is perfect."

"Thank you. I know people think I'm a bit over the top with organizing things, but...," Sydney just shrugged leaving the statement hanging mid-air.

"So, what can I help with?"

"I need to take these 3 million clear beads and fill each of these," Sydney pointed to forty clear vases on the table," about three quarters full."

"Easy enough," Darby leaned down. Standing back up with a smile, "you even have a cool little scoop."

"Yeah, made it so much easier on my dry runs," Sydney said with a chuckle.

Darby filled the first to about three quarters, "This okay?" she asked.

Sydney looked at the vase, "Perfect."

"So, Rachel seems nice," Darby said cautiously.

"She is," Sydney didn't want to discuss Rachel.

"I thought you guys were friends."

"She is more Clementine's friend than mine. But she is nice, and I know she and Lane get along better than he did with Meghan, Clementine's first choice."

"Clementine told me you shot down the first three choices."

Sydney stopped and gaped at Darby.

"One hated kids, one was a man-eater and one is leaving for China in a couple months. I had valid points. What did Clementine tell you?"

Darby grinned at her, "Exactly that."

"You are wrong!" She exclaimed good naturedly rolling her eyes at her friend.

"So it was just my imagination that things seemed a bit strained between Rachel, Lane and yourself tonight?"

"No, this week things have gotten odd, and I'm not certain why. I know Rachel is trying to get to know Sophie and spend time with Lane, but Sophie is going to require time to adjust to new people and routines. I guess I need to back off from seeing her so much. I guess she is too attached…" she could feel the pain invade her heart at the thought.

"You can't allow your relationship with Sophie to be dictated by someone new to the table. So can I ask you a weird question?"

"Sure?"

"Why didn't you and Lane consider dating… each other I mean, before he went and found someone new?"

Sydney swallowed hard at the minefield question Darby had lobbed out into the open. She needed to carefully select her next statement.

"I think he is still just feeling this dating thing out, and… it could get weird. Our friendship… and I'm definitely not his type. You met Rachel. Meghan was just as good looking, and both are blonde. Sarah was blonde. I'm thinking he has a type," she said turning back to continue the task at hand.

"You know, when I was interested in Ryker and he wasn't having anything to do with me, Sarah asked me

Angelica Kate -- 137

if I loved him enough to work things out if he ever did decide to give it a chance."

"And you obviously did," Sydney said with a smile at her friend. She couldn't imagine a more opposite pair in the quiet and solid Ryker and the bubbly happy Darby, but they obviously loved each other beyond words. It was evident to anyone present when they came into a room.

"I did. Do you?"

Sydney turned, certain she had misunderstood the question. "I don't know what you're asking."

"Yes, you do." Darby stood with a hand on her hip waiting.

Sydney looked around to ensure they were alone, and took the time to consider the best way to answer the question.

"Ok, yes…yes I do. Even I didn't realize it until recently, but I do," she whispered.

"Well, then I'm going to give you the same advice Sarah followed that question up with way back when. She told me to march into his office and profess my love for him. Tell him we could work any issues out while making beautiful babies together. And we all know how that worked out," Darby said with a smile rubbing her belly.

"Oh my god! Are you pregnant?" Sydney asked excitedly.

"I am, but no one knows. I don't want to barge in on Clementine's big day, so let that stay between us for a while."

Sydney made a zipper signal with her lips, "your secret is safe with me."

"And now back to you." Darby continued to work through the files as she chatted away. Sydney was unboxing the mirrors that needed to go on the tables below the vases, hoping to avoid the question.

"He is with Rachel…"

"That's just an excuse. I was there tonight as you walked up the aisle during the practice and again at dinner. I would assume that Rachel is struggling right now because she is picking up on the vibes also. Honey, one of you is going to have to break the stalemate. I know Lane is struggling to decide how to proceed with his life, but you and I both know Sarah would approve."

"You don't know…," Sydney looked at Darby without a lick of deception in her eyes.

"I do know. You kept your end of the deal and helped Lane and Sophie through the hardest year of their lives. Sophie already thinks you are her mom. Sarah wanted her family taken care of, and no one I can imagine would do a better job than you. I don't see the downside here."

"You have seen the man, he is a walking Adonis. The women go crazy for him, and while I will say I find

Angelica Kate -- 139

him... you know... I'm just," she waved her hands up and down her body.

"Don't sell yourself..."

"Hey, I know that men find me attractive but not guys like Lane. Please, Darby. I couldn't bear to lose his friendship, or Sophie, or mess up our entire group. It is better this way."

"Okay. I won't bring it up again. I just needed to say my piece on the matter."

"Thank you. Now, boy or girl? What are you hoping for?"

"I have a little boy in Tyler already, so I would love a girl. But Ryker, I think, would prefer boys because he says he knows how to deal with them. And you have met my husband? Getting him out of his comfort level is..." she made a crazy face, "difficult."

Sydney laughed aloud as they continued working side by side. She was feeling less stress and much more accomplishment in short order. Darby and she were able to accomplish a number of the small tasks chatting about all different subjects. It was going to be the best wedding, and she was grateful for the huge part she was able to play. After all, this was her family, not the one she had been born into but the one that mattered most. She would endure anything to make them happy, and she knew each of them would return the favor if called upon to do so. For that she was blessed and never felt short changed. Well, hardly ever.

CHAPTER 10

"Good morning," Lane's mother greeted him with a cup of coffee as he came out of his room the following morning.

"Morning, Mom," he reciprocated, dropping a kiss on his cheek.

"So, I know you went back out last night. Did you go see Rachel?"

"Yeah," he sipped the coffee.

"How did she take it?" she asked, innocently looking at him.

"That was never fun when you did it as a kid," he squinted his eyes at her. "You can't get information out of me by playing dumb any more…I am on to your game."

"So, you broke it off with Rachel. How did she take it?" she sat back with a gloating look on her face.

He shook his head. His mother had always possessed the uncanny ability to read him, and this proved to be no exception.

"She said she saw it coming," he said, gulping coffee and averting his eyes from her knowing gaze.

"Smart girl."

"Mom, just say it. You don't think I'm ready to be dating yet. Well, you are right. I'm done with that for now."

"I didn't say you weren't ready. You're right in thinking Sarah would want you to move on, and I think with the right woman it could be great. You can't force it though, and you and Rachel were definitely never going the distance."

He sighed and sat the mug down.

"Why do you say that? Because Sophie didn't want to go to her last night? She's a baby."

"That isn't what made up my mind. It should never be that much work, and you both looked like you were forcing it last night. I don't care if you are falling in love the first time, widowed and starting over or in any other situation. Love, real love, is a feeling, not a checklist organized to get you to some final destination."

"I know. I figured since it was my second go around, and I still miss Sarah, not like in the beginning, but you know I feel... I justified the fact that it would be harder this time and missed a number of warning signs. She wanted things I wasn't ready for. And Sophie... I think we just take a break and maybe somewhere down the road...," he sighed.

"Meee... maw....," Sophie hollered from the other room.

"My audience calls," his mother said, reaching up and pulling him down for a quick kiss. "I love you son, but sometimes you can't see what is right in front of you," she said, patting his cheek.

He stared after her, not understanding but not willing to press her. She already thought she was smarter than he was, and she had proven it time and again. He was not giving her any reason to gloat further.

Turning toward a warm shower, he was brought to a halt by the shrill of his cellphone.

He picked it up and noticed Darby's name reflected back at him.

"What's up Darby?"

"I need a huge favor," she said, breathless.

"Name it," he said quickly.

"Sydney left the bridal party gifts at her house in a large white shopping bag. In the same bag there are three sets of jewelry for the bridesmaids. I don't want to bother her, as she is a bit crazy today with the details."

"I got it. How quick do you need it?"

"We will begin getting ready in an hour or so," she said hesitantly.

"No problem. I was going to grab a shower and then I can head over there. My mom was going to bring Sophie later, so I can be there soon."

"Sounds good," she said, and without another word disconnected the call.

He took off at a jog for the shower. It seemed like he might need to make himself available for last minute odds and ends. The jewelry might end up being the first but not the last save he was called on to make. He thought with a grin about how keyed up Sydney would be at this point. Anything he could do to alleviate that would be good.

*****

Sydney was a wreck. After only three hours of sleep and now eight hours into what promised to be a long day, she needed a drink. She was at her best organizing events, but even she knew her frayed nerves were on edge. After ensuring all the bridesmaids were starting hair and make-up, she slipped downstairs for a final walk through of the wedding location.

Ten minutes of inspections later, she reassured herself that all centerpieces, chair ties and flowers were perfect. The cake table captured her eyes though. Where was the baker? She frantically searched for her phone, and remembering she left it upstairs, headed that direction.

"Whoa," a strong set of arms stopped her as she rounded the corner.

Looking up she found herself staring at Darby's husband.

"Ryker," she said winding her arms compulsively around the man.

"Ummm... hello to you too," he said clearing his throat.

She brought herself upright, remembering the man didn't like to be hugged. "Sorry, I'm not myself today. I shouldn't have hugged you, but I'm a bit..."

"It's all good. I'm sure since my wife told you our news, you understand how much emotional I'm living with... and don't you dare tell her I said that," he growled. She had known him long enough to know he wasn't scared of his tiny wife and was teasing.

"It's my secret. Is Tyler here?" She hadn't confirmed all the grooms men were in attendance yet, and Tyler was one of the ushers that were still not marked off her check list.

"Yep, little guy was so cute in his suit. He was strutting around like a peacock this morning," he had just a tiny crook of a corner smile as he shared the information.

"I'm sure he looks great," she said inhaling deeply. "I need to go find a baker about…"

"Van just pulled up as I was headed back here."

"Yes!" she said running off, turning around as she remembered her manners. "Thanks!"

He just waved at her.

As she skittered around the corner, she felt her heart hit the floor. The cake being carried was completely the wrong color, "Please let them have delivered the wrong cake," she mumbled looking up for divine intervention.

"Sir, this is not my cake!" she said harsher than she had intended.

"What do you mean? This is the Sorenson wedding," he said in a haughty huff.

"Nope, Benez wedding here," she said almost hysterical.

"Crap! I just delivered the wrong cake. Are you certain…"

"Positive, get me the right cake… now!" She said knowing she was getting a bit hysterical.

"Okay," strong arms came around her. "I think we need to take a break. We need to know in the next ten minutes how you are going to fix this," she heard Lane say over his shoulder, maneuvering her ahead of him and away from the scene of the crime.

"I had it under control," she said quietly.

"I know. I was more worried about him losing a limb," he chuckled.

She turned and glared at him.

"He deserved it. Who delivers the wrong cake to a wedding?" she said on a desperate groan.

"Sweetheart, we have two hours before the wedding and even longer to the reception. I'm sure you scared them enough that they will fix it," he said gently.

"Fine," she said glaring at him. "If they don't, I'm holding you accountable."

"Fair enough." He had the nerve to laugh at her. "But now I have another favor, I need the keys to your house."

"Why?"

"Jewelry and gift pick up," he said tentatively, backing up a bit. "Didn't they say anything to you?"

"No, but now that you mention it…I did forget them. I am batting a thousand today." She jumped up, feeling on the verge of tears. She couldn't keep making mistakes, there was so much to do and she couldn't fall apart now.

"Syd," Lane closed the gap between them and took hold of her shoulders. "Give yourself a break, this is a big circus. Let some of us help."

She took a few steadying breaths. "Thank you, I needed that," she pulled back slightly. "Oh, I wanted to apologize for everything last night. I hope you and Rachel are good... and..."

"Hey, you didn't do anything. It was just... growing pains."

"I know, but..." she started.

"Syd, keys. I gotta run if I'm going to make it back. Oh, and if my mom gets here with Sophie..."

"We got it," she took off at a clip, retrieved the keys and was back down the stairs in less than a minute. Throwing the ring at Lane she turned, "I have a head count to take. Please take the bag up to Darby when you get back."

"Will do," he agreed and was gone.

Glancing at her watch, she decided she needed to hustle. As Maid of Honor she knew that Clementine wouldn't settle for the excuse of lots to do if she marched down the aisle disheveled.

*****

Lane let himself into Sydney's house and immediately set to finding the errant bag of jewelry and gifts. He didn't spot a large shopping bag in the pristine living room. He walked around the corner to her office and again came up empty handed. He trudged down the hall and tried the guest bedroom that was littered with numerous craft project leftovers in the wedding colors. No bag. Finally, he walked out into the hall and stared at her closed bedroom door. *Desperate times* he thought, proceeding to the door and swinging it open.

There on the bed was the treasure he sought. Bounding into the room, he grabbed the bag and headed for the doorway. He stopped as he noticed a picture frame hanging just to the right of her dressing table labeled "family." He instantly acknowledged it wasn't the title or the frame that caught his attention, but rather that one of the pictures was of Sarah. The picture in question was Sarah in the hospital, holding Sophie and smooshed together with a glowing Sydney, taken the day Sophie was born. He had never seen the picture before. He grinned. It was a hospital selfie and so like the hundreds of others Sarah had taken of every detail of life.

Leaning in closer, he took in pictures of Darby and Ryker on their wedding day, and a picture of what he assumed to be Sydney's mom and dad in happier days, prior to their divorce. There was a funny one of Jett, Clementine and Sydney after a robust paintball game. He remembered the day that picture had come in the mail to Jett while deployed. He and Ryker had ribbed Jett about the picture looking like the girls were beating him up. There was a more recent picture of Sophie and him in the bottom frame, and a school picture of Tyler this past year tucked into the corner. Finally, he looked at the large central opening, that wasn't a picture but rather it appeared to be a napkin with writing on it.

He stopped when he saw Sarah's signature at the bottom. He moved in a step to read what was written:

We the wives, friends and girlfriends of our band of brothers – this here is our pact. Should anything ever happen to one of us women, we will step in and fill the gap. It takes a village, and we vow to be each other's tribe…we are FAMILY.

It was signed by Darby, Sydney, Clementine and Sarah. He swiped at the tears welling in his eyes. He couldn't breathe over the lump in his throat as he retraced his footsteps back out the front door.

"I asked for a sign, not a sledgehammer to the heart Sarah," he whispered hoarsely over the lump in his throat.

His brain kept replaying that note over and over in his head, but he was rattled and no coherent thought was processing through the fog.

When he pulled back up at the venue, he was grateful it was Darby that greeted him and not Sydney.

"Hey, I thought…" she said, and then trailed off when she noticed the look on his face. "What's wrong?"

"I just saw something… I… the napkin that Sydney has framed," he stumbled.

"Oh wow, she never showed you before?" Darby said empathetically.

"No! When did you all… why…"

"Whoa boy, calm," she said, looking around to ensure they were alone he assumed.

"It was after the first letter you brought home to Darby. We met up, all of us, and we thought if you guys were thinking so much about us. We needed to have a plan, should something happen to any of us left behind. It was partly a joke, and partly a foundation of what we all have today. Sydney of course took it upon herself to copy and frame it for each of us," she said with a grin.

"Ryker knows about it?"

"Yes. I have mine in the bedroom back home. I'm not certain if Clementine has told Jett yet, but it's not something we hid. We all promised to share parenting duties for any children born, and we are each other's family, Lane. You of all people know that."

"So that is why Sydney stepped up the way she did after Sarah," he sighed rubbing his hand through his hair.

"You've met that woman," Darby chuckled. "She is the fixer, so yes, I think at first that was the reason.

That and the fact that she thought she owed you for Peru... but... somewhere along the way... well, things change."

He looked at her hoping he was understanding, but not willing to risk any more miscommunication.

"You think things changed for her."

"Last night, I gave her some advice your Sarah gave me when I was struggling with missing Ryker after he left the farm the first time," she smiled up at him. "I told Sydney she needed to declare herself to you and fight for what she wants and who she loves. You know Syd, though. I don't think she believes she is good enough for you."

"Why the hell not?" he asked before he could filter the question. Sheepishly looking at Darby, he realizing he had just given his hand away.

She chuckled, "You did decide to start dating other women and told her you needed to remain friends only."

"That was only... thank you," he said bending down to kiss her on the cheek. "I will never ever be able to repay you."

"You have that wrong big guy. This was me paying you back," she said putting her hand on his cheek. "You brought me closure from Bryce, and you sent Ryker back to me when I needed him. I am glad to see I found some small way to thank you for that."

"I have to run," he said clearing his throat.

She took the bag, grinning as he bounded up the stairs. He was running late and tried to figure out from the voices which room the groomsmen were in.

Opening one that didn't have any obvious noises from inside, he stopped dead in his tracks when asked, "Can you please help me zip this?"

*****

Sydney had bullied through the poking and prodding of having her make-up done but having a room full of women watch as she tried to change was not happening. Slipping next door, she had shimmied out of her street clothes and into the form fitting pastel pink concoction. It fit like a second skin but the zipper was problematic as it started below her fanny and needed to go up even with her shoulder blades. When the door opened, she assumed one of the nosy bridesmaids had entered.

"Can you please help me zip this?"

"You and that damn dress," Lane said, as she heard the door closing.

Her breath caught and she twisted around, her hand at her heart.

"I thought you were someone else," she said hoping the heat in her face didn't melt her fresh make-up.

He took several more steps forward rather than retreating, further elevating her blood pressure.

"You need to be getting ready yourself," she said gulping in fresh air, her eyes never straying from his.

"I will. I thought you needed help…" he said with a lopsided grin, closing the rest of the distance between them.

"I don't think your girlfriend would appreciate you helping me get dressed." She heard her voice crack despite trying to remain calm and rationale.

"If I still had a girlfriend, I'm certain that would be the case."

"What happened?"

"I think we both came to the realization it was a bad fit. Besides, I kept having thoughts about doing this," he pulled her toward him and kissed her just below her ear. "And this…" his lips moved to the throbbing beat in the hollow of her neck.

"Lane," she whimpered.

"You don't like," he asked leaning back to examine her face with an innocent glint to his eyes.

"I like," she whispered after a pregnant pause.

"Thank god," he said as his other hand snaked from his side to her backside dragging her hard up against him.

She immediately wrapped one arm around pulling him closer, moaning her further approval as his lips met hers. She moved the other hand up to his massive chest and down his arm, loving the journey. With each inch she felt herself coming further apart.

He lifted his head for just a moment, "Syd, I'm so sorry…"

"Shut-up," she said dragging him back down. She couldn't risk him coming to his senses and ending the blissful interlude.

He growled in his throat in response, and utilizing his tongue fully initiated himself to her mouth. She could not remember a single instant when she had felt so happy and needy at the same time.

"God, you are so beautiful," he said against the top of her head. He was having trouble catching his breath.

"I know I'm not, please don't say…"

"Syd, quit selling yourself short. If we didn't have to be at a wedding in a little while, I would show you just how beautiful I find everything about you."

"Oh my god!" Darby's voice from the entry put a stop to any further conversation.

"What's wrong?" Clementine, dressed in white was pushing through the door.

"What's all the yelling about?" Ryker's voice joined in the general hubbub.

"Is everyone invited to this party?" Jett laughed.

Angelica Kate -- 157

Sydney's face was beet red as she took in her friends all crowded around - a devoted band of brothers and the women who loved them.

Excerpt
A Soldier's Promise
Also by Angelica Kate

PROLOGUE

Ryker pushed himself up and looked around for the other members of his team, the sound of the explosion still pounding in his head. He couldn't hear anything above the ringing in his ears, but was determined to find the others. He swiped the blood away from his eyes, and wiped his hand on his uniform. He knew that a piece of metal had ripped at his head and could feel his left arm nearly wrenched from the socket when he was slammed to the ground. He couldn't focus on his own injuries, as he was able to move and needed to find his men and get everyone to safety.

He felt relief flow over him, as he watched Jett and Lane moving toward him bent low to the ground. Both men kept scanning their surroundings, not certain if the single explosion was a solitary event or merely the first in a series. He saw Jett's face register emotion as he glanced past Ryker, and then make eye contact causing Ryker's gut to clench. Slowly he turned and saw Bryce, the fourth member of their elite team, lying a few feet away in distress. The slight gurgling noises emanating from his mouth, and the blood oozing from a wound around his midsection, caused Ryker to forget his own safety as he lunged in Bryce's direction. He half crawled half ran to Bryce, he needed to get the bleeding stopped and get him out of the open.

"Don't move, Bry. Don't move, Buddy." His trained eyes darted in every direction keeping a watchful eye, as he applied intense pressure to Bryce's wound.

Lane and Jett scuttled over and took in the scene.

"We need to get out of here," Lane said as Jett turned to protect them from any enemies.

"Ryker..." he heard Bryce's labored voice.

"Don't talk, Bry. Save your strength," he said soothingly.

"It's no good...remember...." Bryce gasped for breath, and reached out to grab Ryker's shirt. "Your promise...remem..."

"I remember," he said to Bryce. "But you are going to make it home to Darby."

"Ry, we need to move now!" Jett screamed.

"You guys move out," Ryker hissed. "Stay low."

The mission had been completely successful up until five minutes ago. They had destroyed the stronghold of a known terrorist cell, and gotten back out unseen. At least that was what they had believed. They were less than two miles from their pickup site, and had been sensing freedom with Ryker bringing up the rear. All that had changed in a heartbeat when the rocket exploded in front of them, knocking them all about.

The team was very professional. Lane gave Bryce one last look and took his position to provide cover out of this god forsaken hellhole. Ryker wouldn't have anyone else out here with him. They had done numerous operations together, and worked like a well-oiled machine, each anticipating and covering the others' movements. Ryker took one last look at Bryce, whose eyes stared lifeless at the sky. This was the first loss for the team, and it wouldn't be easy to recover from. He moved his hands over Bryce's eyes, said a silent prayer, leaned over, and hoisted the limp body over his good shoulder. Mentally, he registered the pain the exertion was causing, but blocked it out. *No one got left behind.*

Bending under the weight of his responsibilities, he ducked and ran behind the cover that Jett and Lane provided. Two miles, and they would all be going home.

CHAPTER 1

Six months later

Darby was working hard to get the rows cleaned up in the oversized garden. The weeds needed to be removed, lettuce cut, and some of the beans culled out. She would have some help in a couple of hours from the season staff she had hired, but she liked getting out in the early morning light and tending to the garden on her own. It gave her time to think alone, with nothing but her own thoughts.

It was in those quiet moments that she talked to Bryce, and attempted to reconcile her future without him.

She missed him as much today as six months ago when THAT letter had been delivered by the uniformed officer and a chaplain. Details about his demise in some war zone thousands of miles away were sketchy, as his mission had been highly classified. The details wouldn't make her feel any better though. He was forever gone, and would never again hold her in his arms, or see the gorgeous farm that had been their mutual dream. The uniformed officers had offered their thanks on behalf of a grateful nation for his service, and platitudes for his loss. What they hadn't been able to give her was even a shard of an idea of what she was to do now that he wasn't ever coming home.

They had been high school sweethearts and become engaged before he shipped out the first time. In every fantasy, he had been her Prince Charming, the one who would truly make all her dreams a reality. He wasn't coming home for their wedding though, and her fairy tale had abruptly ended without the happily ever after. Not one to sit and cry over spilled milk, she carried on with the help of her parents, a growing staff, and a love for the business she was running. She had hired help for the horse training and therapy classes she offered. A farm overseer saw to the bean, lettuce, celery, and strawberry fields, the surplus produce of which she sold to local markets.

When Darby was a junior in college, she and her mother had jointly inherited the property from her grandmother that had been in the family for two generations. Right after graduation, she and her parents had put into play the big plans she had for the farm. They had also started planning her wedding to Bryce. For a moment, her sight blurred. It was exactly two weeks until the day that she had planned for so carefully, and as it grew closer, she allowed herself some wallowing. She felt the weight of grief much heavier on her soul in recent days, more than even that original sharp stabbing pain when she had seen the car pull up and knew, even before she heard it, what the news would be. Perhaps she had been numb then.

Bryce had known the inherent risks of his job, but from as early as she could remember, he had been devotedly committed to serving his country. Almost as much as the farm was her dream, the military was his, and they had supported each other in equal measure. Even knowing how their story would end, Darby would not have done anything differently. It had been his destiny, and keeping him at home would have been an unhappy unfulfilled existence for him. He was with her now, and had died doing what he loved. In that, he was luckier than a lot of people she knew.

As she turned her face to the orange ball of sun on the horizon, she felt Bryce around her.

"Gorgeous day," she said to him. "I miss you today. Just a couple of weeks and I would have been your wife. I hope you are home and happy, and I'm trying every day to be the same," she whispered.

On the whisper of the wind, she swore that she could feel his embrace.

She turned and opened her eyes when she heard the car approaching along the drive. It was a newer SUV style, and she didn't recognize it, which was rare in her small town. She knew everyone, and few visited this early. She stood, shielding her eyes and waiting.

*****

Lane kept his attention on the road ahead of him, as he was unfamiliar with the dirt road they now traveled. He had made the promise months earlier to take this trip. He remembered the moment with clarity as if yesterday, but not for a moment had he been expecting the chip to be called in. He and his wife, Sarah, were making the trek to see Bryce's fiancée Darby. He had never met the woman, but he felt like he knew her from all the stories that Bryce had told him. He and Bryce, along with Ryker and Jett, had been a close-knit team and had walked through hell together in the service to their country. They had been through so many missions that he had lost count, but that last one was different. Bryce hadn't made it out alive, and Ryker hadn't been cleared yet back to active duty after surgery on his arm. Jett and he had been luckier physically, but mentally, the moment that blast had ripped apart his life still constantly played out vividly in his nightmares.

He had been the one to bring Bryce's body home. Ryker and Jett had both been hospitalized and not able to make the trip. He was the only married one of the group, and had needed to hug his wife. To reassure him that somewhere the inhumanity he worked around daily was balanced by the one woman who kept him tethered to his softer side. She was the picture he carried, the reason he fought, and the person he wanted to come home to while Jett and Ryker preferred to remain busy. Bryce had been fortunate to have that same type of connection with Darby, and it was something that had deeply bonded them together. He couldn't even imagine what Darby was going through, and was grateful that it wasn't his beloved Sarah having to experience such loss.

Sarah tightly squeezed his hand as he put the vehicle in park, pulling him out of his reverie. The farm was exactly as Bryce had described it, complete with a picturesque lovely old farmhouse and well organized gardens. He looked around and saw the horses Bryce had been so proud of, contentedly grazing in deep green fields. He inhaled deeply and took it all in.

"It's going to be okay," Sarah said. "I know I would have wanted to see one of your friends, and know what happened if it was me. Besides, I've never been to this particular amusement park, it should be fun," she smiled at him.

He loved that she truly understood, and that she kept him grounded. Whenever he came back from a difficult mission, she was patient while he took the time to decompress. Sarah had been his high school sweetheart, just as Bryce had been Darby's. He looked at his wife, and couldn't fathom how hard it must be for Darby to go on, knowing that Bryce was never coming home. Military spouses, girlfriends, and the like were a special breed. Strong and secure in their ability to carry the weight when the other partner took on serving a higher calling. He was fortunate to have one of the good ones right beside him. Something he wished for Jett and Ryker, who struggled to overcome and process while surrounded only by military bad boys.

Darby was walking in their direction. He would recognize her anywhere from the pictures Bryce had repeatedly shown them. She had written nearly every other day when they were deployed, sent little care packages to be shared with the group, and served as Bryce's strong anchor to life in the States. More than once, he had found Bryce rereading letters from Darby in the dark of night after something had gotten particularly dicey during one of their maneuvers.

He slowly exited the vehicle, gripping the packet of letters. He looked at the still unopened one on top, remembering the agreement he had made with Bryce. The contents of that last private letter were completely unknown. He blinked back tears that threatened as Darby finished her trek to him. Standing a few feet apart, she sized him up.

"You military?"

"Yes ma'am. I'm Lane Grettner and this is my wife Sarah," he indicated Sarah still sitting in the car. She slowly exited, as if unsure what to do.

"Lane?" Darby looked confused, and when her eyes alighted on the letters she rapidly returned her gaze to his face. Her eyes were glistening. "Those are my Bryce's."

"Yes ma'am. I was asked by him to do him a solid and return them to you, and this one," he pulled the fresh sealed letter from the top and extended it to her, "was mine to deliver personally. I am so sorry for your loss." His own tears were making his voice hoarse, and he cleared his throat to gain control. "He was a brother in arms and I miss him every day."

She opened her arms, and he stepped forward. "I miss him so much. Thank you," she said as her arms encircled him.

After a moment, she stepped back and stared down at the envelope. "Do you know what it says? The front says to read it out loud with you."

"Yes ma'am. I don't know what it says, but he did make me promise a special outing. I'm sure he explains it."

She looked at Sarah and gave a teary smile. Finally returning to the letter, she inhaled sharply and slid her finger through the seal. Pulling the paper slowly out, and unfolding the single sheet.

A fresh round of tears spilled over as she saw the familiar scrawl. In a soft voice, she began to read:

Dear Darby,

If you are reading this, it means that something went wrong. Please don't focus on that, or let it define you. I loved you enough for an entire lifetime, and will forever be grateful to you for the childhood, dreams, and goals we shared. I need you to promise this will only be a single chapter in a life fully lived, as you promised me that night before I left. In order to force you forward to that future, I've made Lane promise to visit you. It has been six months since I went home to the Lord, so it is time.

I know you well enough to believe that you are throwing yourself into work at growing the farm and probably haven't done a fun thing since you got word I was gone. I'm going to request that you get your mom and dad to watch the farm for a day, and take a road trip. I asked Lane to ensure that you go have some fun. You and Lane can swap stories about me. Sarah his beautiful bride and you have a lot in common, so I think you will certainly find something to gab about. Make this a dying wish of mine.

Adventure Land was something we always talked about -- taking a day road trip to see, and riding every roller coaster. Sweetheart, take that road trip with Lane and Sarah.

I love you and will always watch over you....go have fun you three!

Love, Bryce

She sat staring at the letter for so long, Lane turned to Sarah who held up her hands in a gesture to indicate patience. When Darby did look up again, she threw herself at him, hugging him so tight that he was short of breath.
"Thank you!"